Dear Reader,

Elena Cabrera, illegitimate daughter of Bravo family patriarch Davis Bravo is ready for love. Builder Rogan Murdoch is ready for his freedom. Finally.

Rogan's parents died tragically when he was barely an adult and not only did he take over the family business, Murdoch Homes, but he also became guardian and stand-in parent to his three younger siblings. It hasn't been an easy time. But he and his family made it through. Now, the last of his charges, his baby sister, is off to college in the fall. And he's looking forward to being footloose at last.

But then he meets Elena. The attraction is instant. And powerful. But he knows she's not the kind of woman who'll go for a casual affair. And that's all he's ready for right now.

He should stay away from her. Far, far away.

But somehow, fate keeps throwing them together. And every time he sees her, it's harder for him to resist her— let alone remember all the reasons he needs to be free.

Happy reading everyone,

Christine Rimmer

MARRIAGE, BRAVO STYLE!

CHRISTINE RIMMER

SPECIAL EDITION

Published by Silhouette Books

America's Publisher of Contemporary Romance

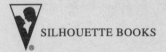

SILHOUETTE BOOKS

ISBN-13: 978-0-373-65583-0

Recycling programs
for this product may
not exist in your area.

MARRIAGE, BRAVO STYLE!

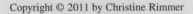

Books by Christine Rimmer

CHRISTINE RIMMER

came to her profession the long way around. Before settling down to write about the magic of romance, she'd been everything from an actress to a salesclerk to a waitress. Now that she's finally found work that suits her perfectly, she insists she never had a problem keeping a job—she was merely gaining "life experience" for her future as a novelist. Christine is grateful not only for the joy she finds in writing, but for what waits when the day's work is through: a man she loves, who loves her right back, and the privilege of watching their children grow and change day to day. She lives with her family in Oklahoma. Visit Christine at www.christinerimmer.com.

To our families.
They drive us crazy
and teach us what life is all about.

Chapter One

"Elena, I don't know how to say this…"

"Say what?" Carefully, so not too much filling would spill out, Elena Cabrera lifted a taco off her plate.

"I've met someone else."

Elena had her mouth wide open to take a bite. Instead, she eased the taco back down to the plate. Then she put her hands in her lap and stared across the cozy corner table at totally hunky Antonio Aguilar.

So much for going on the pill, she thought.

They'd been dating for two months now. She'd started on the pill two weeks ago. Because she'd been really, really hoping that Tonio would be the one.

"You're a beautiful woman, Elena." His dark-chocolate eyes were full of regret. "I don't know why we never really clicked…."

Clicked. They hadn't clicked. Was that the problem?

Something was. She was twenty-five years old and still a virgin.

Nothing against being a virgin, per se. Until not all that long ago, being a virgin had been her choice. Men *had* made advances. She'd turned down every one.

After all, she was a woman of principle. She'd been saving herself for true love. Seriously. True, forever love. Like her sister, Mercy, had with Luke.

Like her parents had.

Or like she'd always thought they had.

But then, three years ago, she'd learned that her darling *Papi* wasn't her biological father, after all. Her father's sworn enemy, Davis Bravo, was. Her mom had been lying to her dad for all these years, letting him believe that Elena was his. Letting *Elena* believe it, too.

Needless to say, her dad and her mom weren't together anymore.

So much for true, forever love.

"Elena." Tonio leaned toward her across his untouched plate. He looked more than a little annoyed. "Have you heard a single word I said?"

"Uh, yeah. It's not working out. You've found someone else."

"This is pretty much the whole problem. You know that, don't you?"

"This?"

"This." He said a bad word in Spanish under his breath and made a sweeping gesture with his lean brown hand, his sculpted cheekbones flushed with color. He was definitely not happy with her. "You."

"Me."

"You. Elena, when we're together, you act like you're a thousand miles away." He pushed his plate toward the center of the table with a look of pure disdain. "And now

I've met Tappy, well, there's no comparison. Tappy adores me. A man needs that, to know that his woman is there for him, that he has her absolute undivided attention when he speaks."

"Wait a minute. Tappy. Her name is Tappy?"

He made a hissing sound between his gorgeous white teeth, and looked away. "Now you make fun of her name. A woman cares for me. *Really* cares. And you make fun of her name." More Spanish swear words ensued.

"Tonio. Come on…" Now she felt guilty—which made no sense. He was breaking up with her. And *she* felt guilty…?

"No." He showed her the palm of his hand. "It's enough. I don't know why I was so worried about telling you. It's not as if you care."

"Tonio, please…"

"It's over. Finished."

"Well, I know that. You said that. But couldn't we at least—?"

"Stop." He took out his wallet, threw some bills on the table. "You never respected me. You never *wanted* me." He swept to his feet. "Well, I have a real woman now. Goodbye, Elena."

And with a scornful toss of his proud dark head, he was gone.

Elena didn't watch him go. She picked up the taco again and finished her lunch, her gaze studiously on her plate. If people were staring, she didn't want to know. The whole situation was embarrassing enough as it was.

Not only had she lost Antonio, she didn't feel all that bad about it.

Was there something wrong with her? Sometimes she really did wonder.

Her cell rang as she stood at the cash register paying the check. It was her sister.

Mercy said, "Hey."

Elena signaled to the hostess that the five dollars in change should go to the waiter and smiled at the sound of her sister's voice. "Hey." She turned for the glass doors that led to the parking lot.

"Did you hear?" Mercy asked. "Dad thinks he's found a buyer for the company." Their father was a builder. He owned and ran Cabrera Construction. Lately, he'd been making noises that he wanted to retire. Mercy added, "Some friend of Caleb's, I think."

Caleb was one of Davis Bravo's seven sons, and thus Elena's half brother. He was also Mercy's brother-in-law, since Mercy's husband, Luke, was another of Davis's sons.

Family connections. Truly convoluted, at least when it came to the Bravos and the Cabreras. It wasn't quite as creepy as it might sound, though. Mercy, unlike Elena, was not related by blood to the Bravos—or the Cabreras, for that matter. Mercy had been adopted into the Cabrera family when she was twelve.

Elena reached her car and pulled open the door. "I remember now. Caleb mentioned that some guy he knows in Dallas—Logan somebody-or-other?—might be interested." In the past few years, after the big revelation concerning Elena's true parentage, Elena and Caleb had become not only newfound siblings, but close friends, as well.

"Not Logan," said Mercy. "Rogan. Rogan Murdoch."

"Rogan. Right." Elena slid in behind the wheel and started the engine to get the air-conditioning going. April in San Antonio could be as hot as August in other places. "Caleb said the guy runs his family's company."

"Murdoch Homes," Mercy confirmed. "And he want-to expand. He showed up yesterday. And he's with Dad now...."

"With Dad at the office?"

"That's what *Papi* said when I called."

Elena readjusted the vent so the cold air blasted into her face. It felt good. "You think I should go over there? Check the guy out?"

Mercy laughed. "I would do it myself, but I have a sick heifer to treat." Mercy was a large-animal vet. "And then I have to get home to take Lucas to Mommy and Me." Lucas was her two-year-old. And she was two months pregnant with her and Luke's second baby.

True love, a toddler and a baby on the way. Mercy had it all. Elena adored her big sister. Otherwise, she would be green with envy.

"I'll take care of it." She bent closer to the vent so the cool air flowed down the front of her shirt. "It's Good Friday. What else have I got to do?" Elena taught middle-school social studies. Good Friday was a school holiday.

"You sure? I thought you mentioned something about lunch with Antonio...."

"Oh." Elena slumped back in the seat and stared glumly out the windshield. "That."

Mercy made a low, sympathetic sound. "What happened?"

"I just got dumped over fish tacos."

"No."

"Yeah."

"Are you all right?"

"Sadly, yes. I'm just fine."

"Oh, *chica*..."

"Tonio's found someone else."

"That bastard."

"Her name is Tappy."

"Tappy?"

"It's what I said—and I can hear you laughing."

"Tappy?"

"Stop it, Mercedes." But Mercy didn't stop. And then Elena was laughing, too.

Finally, Mercy pulled herself together enough to remark philosophically, "Well, at least your heart isn't broken over this."

"Yeah. It's really depressing."

"Elena." Her sister's voice was gentle, soothing. "There's someone out there for you. I know there is."

"Keep talking. I'm twenty-five. I've never been in love—not that I'm feeling sorry for myself or anything."

"What's this never? What about Roberto Pena?"

"That was high school. It's been a decade, in case you didn't notice."

"It will happen. You'll see."

Enough of the pity party. Elena sat forward again and reached for the ignition key. "Gotta go. Got to check out this Rogan character, make sure *Papi* knows what he's doing."

"Hit me back. Let me know what you think of him."

Cabrera Construction took up half a block in a street of auto repair shops and contractor supply outlets. Years and years ago, the place had been a used car lot, so it had plenty of parking surrounding the flat-roofed central structure, which was the former showroom. It had big windows in front and a giant reception area, with a warren of hallways and office space in back. Behind the main building, there was more parking and also four large sheds where Elena's dad stored equipment and building supplies that weren't currently needed on a job.

Elena pulled in next to her dad's giant shiny red extended

cab. There were three other vehicles parked in the same row. One was her dad's secretary's car. One belonged to another Cabrera Construction employee.

There was also a Mercedes she'd never seen before. It was low and lean and fast-looking. A beautiful silver bullet of a car.

As she entered the building that her dad had owned for almost twenty years now, she thought how sad it was that he might actually sell out. She had memories here. Family memories. From back when her mom and dad were still together and so much in love it was kind of embarrassing.

If she closed her eyes and listened real hard, she could almost hear her own happy laughter as she and Mercy played tag or hide-and-seek.

> *"Tag, you're it!" Mercy would crow in big-sister triumph.*
> *"No fair!" Elena would whine.*
> *"Is so!"*
> *"Papi, Mercy cheated...."*
> *"Don't be such a baby." Mercy would stick out her tongue. "Did not."*
> *"Did so!"*

Elena opened her eyes. The memory of young voices receded. Yes, it was sad to think of someone else running the place, someone else's children playing tag in the reception area.

But then again, neither of Javier Cabrera's daughters had shown any interest in following in his footsteps. Elena was a teacher, Mercy a vet. And there was no son. Her dad was close to sixty and he often complained that he was tired, ready to relax a little, maybe travel some, see the world.

If this thing with Caleb's friend panned out, her dad

might get his chance for freedom. Too bad he no longer had her mom to share his retirement with.

He really ought to get out more, Elena thought. He ought to try and meet someone. But he never did. He and her mom were over and done with. But they were true Catholics. They might be apart with no hope for a reconciliation, but there would be no one else for either of them.

Really, it was kind of heartbreaking.

But she shouldn't think like that. Maybe they would surprise her, and each of them would end up happy with someone else.

It could happen. Lately, even though she dreaded the thought of dealing with a stepmother or stepfather, she found herself wishing for one. Hadn't her parents suffered enough? Elena thought so. They both ought to just move on....

"Elena." Marcella, who had been her dad's secretary for as long as Elena could remember, smiled a greeting from behind the front desk.

"Hi. Is my dad in back?"

The secretary nodded and then tipped her big head of red hair toward the hallway that led to Javier's private office and the drafting room. She pitched her voice low. "He's with the buyer."

The buyer. So was the sale already made, then? "Is it all right if I go back, you think?"

Marcella shrugged. "I don't see why not."

Elena hesitated. "I wouldn't want to interrupt anything important. What if they're in the middle of delicate negotiations?" And then she heard voices—her dad's and another man's.

Marcella smiled again. "No problem. They're coming out, anyway."

"Elena," her dad said a moment later as he and another

taller, younger man emerged from the hallway to the back rooms. Her dad gave her a warm, tired-looking smile.

They'd come a long way from those first awful days when he'd learned that she wasn't his natural daughter. There had been a time when he could hardly bear to look at her. He'd hated himself for that. But she'd never held it against him. She'd understood his pain. After all, she had lived through that same pain herself.

And slowly, they'd become what they really were again. Father and daughter, blood tie or not.

She went to him and he wrapped his strong arms around her. He smelled of everything safe and good in the world, like Old Spice aftershave and geraniums in the sun. "*Papi,*" she whispered. "I just thought I'd stop by."

"I'm glad." He released her. She gazed up at him, thinking he looked so old, all of a sudden. The crow's feet at the corners of his black eyes were etched so deep they seemed to make his whole face droop. Her dear *Papi.* Old. When had that happened? "Elena, this is Rogan Murdoch."

She turned to the other man, her gaze tracking up his broad, deep chest to a very Irish-looking face with green eyes and straight brows, full lips, a square jaw and a strong nose that looked like it had been broken at least once. He wasn't handsome, exactly. But he was certainly compelling. And very…male.

He smiled at her and took her hand. "Elena," he said, as if he knew her already. As if he'd only been waiting for her to show up. Her throat felt dry. She gulped. Words completely eluded her. "Caleb's mentioned you often." His large, warm hand engulfed hers. She couldn't breathe—or more precisely, she *wasn't* breathing. She had to consciously suck in a breath and push it back out again. "We're just going to lunch," he said. "Why don't you join us?"

She eased her hand free of his. It seemed safer, somehow,

not to be touching him. At the same time, she had the presence of mind to glance down, to check out his other hand.

He had thick, strong fingers. And he wore no wedding band.

She managed weakly, "I already ate, thanks."

"Come with us, anyway," her dad said from behind her. "Have a cold drink, maybe a piece of pie."

"Well, I..."

"Yeah. Please," Rogan said, in his deep, rich, slightly rough voice that sent a lovely shiver racing under the surface of her skin. "Join us."

She couldn't have said no if her life had depended on it.

Chapter Two

At lunch, Rogan sat across from Javier and his daughter. The restaurant was on the River Walk. They had a table out on the patio overlooking the water and the tour boats gliding past.

But the best view was across the table from Rogan. He tried not to stare.

The Cabrera girl was beautiful. Too beautiful. Mess-with-a-man's-head beautiful.

She had thick coffee-colored hair that fell around her slim shoulders in soft waves, hair shot through with strands of red and gold. It was the kind of hair that made a man's fingers itch to touch it. And beyond all that amazing hair, she had golden brown eyes and a mouth made for kissing.

And her skin. Soft. Velvety. Golden as the rest of her. Somehow, he couldn't seem to tear his eyes off that dimple that appeared at the corner of her mouth when she smiled.

Rogan was not a poetic man. But when he looked at Elena Cabrera, he heard poems in his head.

It was an acute case of lust at first sight.

And lust was fine. Lust was great. With somebody other than Javier Cabrera's daughter. Somebody who didn't happen to be Caleb Bravo's adored half sister.

Rogan could tell just by looking at her that she wasn't going to be interested in a simple, mutually satisfying hookup. She would want at least the potential for a serious romance. Marriage would have to be a possibility.

And it wasn't. Not for Rogan. Not for years yet.

He saw freedom in his immediate future and he intended to enjoy it.

Javier said, "I understand that you and Caleb went to school together?"

Rogan smiled at the older man. Time to trot out the family history, clarify the personal connections. "Yes, we did. UT in Austin. He introduced me to Victor Lukovic. Victor had come to the U.S. on a football scholarship. Now he plays football for the Dallas Cowboys. We hung out together for a while, the three of us—Caleb, Victor and me."

Elena told her father, "Victor and Caleb's wife, Irina, were raised together in Argovia—it's a small country in the Balkans, on the Adriatic Sea."

"Ah," said Javier. "That's right. I remember now." He glanced across at Rogan again. "Caleb gave Irina a job as his housekeeper, so she could get a permit to work in the U.S. They fell in love and married."

"That's right."

"And Victor is a linebacker. They call him the Balkan Bear."

"The one and only," Rogan said. "Since he and his family live in the Dallas area, we get together often."

"So you all three graduated from UT the same year?"

"No. Caleb was a year ahead of Victor and me. And I left in my junior year, so I never did get my degree."

Javier frowned. "What happened that you didn't graduate?"

"My parents were killed in a freak boating accident. I went home and took over the family business."

Javier's daughter made a soft sound of distress. "Oh, Rogan. How awful for you...."

"How old were you?" Javier asked.

"Twenty-one."

"So young to be in charge of your own company..."

He shook his head. "The death of my parents, that was bad. They should have had years and years ahead of them. But taking over the business? It was no hardship. It was something I wanted to do. I'd been working with my dad every summer for years before he died. I knew the business. And my plan had always been to go in with my dad eventually, to take over when he was ready to retire."

"I lost my father when I was twenty," said Javier. The dark circles under his eyes gave him a haunted look just then. "It's not a good thing, for a man to lose the steadying hand of a father too soon. It can make him...bitter. Impatient. Angry."

Rogan met Javier's eyes without flinching. "I managed. I got through it. I don't think I'm bitter."

Javier shook his head and muttered regretfully, "I spoke of myself, not of you."

"Ah," Rogan said, and left it at that.

Elena was looking at her father now. *"Papi,"* she said softly, and touched his shoulder, a consoling sort of touch.

Javier gave her a gentle smile. And then he spoke to Rogan again. "And didn't you tell me you had brothers and a sister?"

"Cormac and Niall are twenty-four and twenty-three respectively. Cormac works with me. We're partners. I run the jobs. He runs the finances and acts as my second on-site when necessary. Niall is in law school. My baby sister, Brenda, is eighteen and headed off to college back east in the fall."

"They're all doing well, then?"

"Yes, they are."

"Who cared for them, when you lost your mother and father?"

"I did."

The older man regarded him for several long seconds. At last, he nodded. "You are an admirable man."

Rogan didn't feel all that admirable. "I did what I had to do."

"No," said Javier. "You did the right thing at a difficult time. In the end, family is what matters. And you thought of your family when many would have only cared for themselves. I respect that, greatly. I wish…" He looked away.

Elena leaned toward her father. Rogan thought she would say something to the older man—something comforting, maybe. But then she only put her hand on his arm.

Javier patted her hand and gave her another of those gentle smiles.

The waiter came with their food. After that, they spoke mostly of the various projects Javier's company had in the works and of how both men viewed the transition should they reach an agreement.

Elena didn't say much through the meal. She sipped the iced tea she'd ordered and laughed a couple of times, once at a wry joke Javier made, once at some remark of Rogan's. Her laughter was low and rich. It sent a thrill through him, a kind of vibration that brought with it a feeling of promise.

Of anticipation.

As a rule, Rogan was a strictly disciplined man. He'd had to be, after his parents were gone. He made decisions and he stuck by them.

He'd made a decision about Elena the first moment he saw her: hands off. But when she laughed in that way of hers and when that dimple tucked itself in so temptingly beside her full mouth, well, he didn't feel all that disciplined. He felt he stood on the brink of something heady and fine.

And all he wanted was a little shove, just enough to give himself permission to jump.

"Well?" Mercy said without even a hello. "You didn't call me back."

It was after five and Elena was at home, in her office at her condo, grading papers. She tucked the phone against her shoulder and set down her red marker. "You said you had Mommy and Me."

"That was then. We got home two hours ago. But anyway. What did you think of Rogan Murdoch?"

"I liked him. There's something…solid about him. And I think Dad likes him a lot."

"But is Dad actually going to sell to him?"

"Nothing was said either way while I was with them— but yeah, that's the feeling I get."

"Wow." Mercy made a low, disbelieving sound. "Really?"

"Mmm-hmm."

"Dad. Retired. It's hard to imagine." Mercy's voice held a note of sadness. "And I can't quite get my mind around the idea of Cabrera Construction belonging to someone else. I mean, sometimes it seems as though our past, together, as a family…it's just slowly fading away."

Elena knew exactly what her sister was talking about. "I

hear you. It's depressing. But still. I can see it happening, see Dad selling, now I've met Rogan."

"So what's he look like?"

"Big. Irish." Elena stared into the middle distance, conjuring up the sight of him. "He has these beautiful green eyes. Irish eyes, you know? Like that old song…"

Mercy chuckled. "You *really* liked him."

She might play coy with someone else. But never with Mercy. "Yeah. I really did."

"Did he ask you out?"

I wish. "Oh, come on. I just met him."

"Well. Did he like you, too?"

If you can't tell the truth to your own sister, who *can* you tell it to? Plus, Mercy wouldn't say a word to anyone else. When it came to romance, the two of them had a longstanding vow to keep each other's confidences. "I think he did like me. Yeah."

"Come to dinner at the ranch Sunday," Mercy said— out of nowhere, it seemed to Elena. By "the ranch," Mercy meant the Bravo family ranch, Bravo Ridge, which was a little ways out of town going north, on the southern edge of the Hill Country. Once Bravo Ridge had belonged to the Cabreras. But back in the 1950s, James Bravo had won it off Emilio Cabrera in a horse race, setting off decades of feuding between the families.

The feud was over now.

More or less.

And Mercy, Luke and little Lucas lived at Bravo Ridge together. Luke ran the place. And just about every Sunday they had a big family dinner there. Davis Bravo—who was the oldest son of James—and his wife, Aleta, had had nine children. The siblings and their families tried to show up for Sunday dinner at the ranch at least every couple of months or so.

"Now, there's my idea of a great time," Elena said wryly. "Easter Sunday dinner with the sperm donor and family."

"You've got to quit calling him that," Mercy chided.

Elena laughed. "I always call him that. And you always tell me I have to stop."

"You need to make peace with him."

"Mercy, I don't care if you are my big sister. Don't lecture me, okay?"

"He *is* your father."

"*Papi* is my father. And can we not have this argument again, please?"

"You've forgiven Mom," Mercy prodded reproachfully. Lately, she was getting like a dog with a favorite bone on this subject. She just wouldn't let go. "And think about it…"

"I'd rather not."

Mercy kept after her anyway. "*Mami* did worse than Davis. Davis confessed to Aleta that he'd had an affair. And he never even knew you were his daughter for all those years. Why can't you forgive him?"

"Mom is…my mother."

"And Davis is—"

"Uh-uh. Don't say it again. Just let it be. I mean it. Please?"

Mercy drew in an audible breath and blew it out hard. "All right. I'm done. At least for now—but say you'll come to Sunday dinner."

With waning patience, Elena reminded her, "I thought you just said you were done."

"I am. I'm not asking you to come for Davis's sake. I'm asking because Caleb and Irina are coming. And Mr. Irish Eyes is staying with them…."

Rogan was staying with Caleb and Irina.

And he would be at the ranch on Sunday.

Elena's heart rate accelerated and she felt slightly breathless.

Stunned, she put a hand against her chest. How lovely, to simply *think* of a certain man and get that rising feeling inside.

At last.

She asked, sounding as breathless as she felt, "He's coming to dinner Sunday? Why didn't you *tell* me?"

Mercy chuckled. "You didn't give me a chance. You started right in about Davis. So. You'll come?"

Elena considered the pros and cons. Getting to see Rogan again versus having to be around the sperm donor. It took her about half a second to make her choice. "Fine. I'm there."

She'd barely hung up from talking to Mercy when Caleb called.

Her favorite brother asked, "How about dinner tomorrow night, at my house?"

Her heart was getting a workout. Now, it did a happy dance. Rogan was staying with Caleb, so he would most likely be there for dinner tomorrow.

Another chance to see him. She grinned like an idiot. Why shouldn't she grin? No one was watching. "Love to," she said.

"You're so easy," Caleb teased.

"Well, I do like your wife a lot. And I'm willing to put up with you."

"I was afraid you maybe had a date with Antonio."

"Uh, no. Antonio and I have decided to…move on."

Caleb was a salesman by nature and by trade, the top producer at BravoCorp, the family company. He usually knew just the right thing to say. This situation was no exception. He went directly to the assumption that it must have been Elena who had done the dumping. "Poor guy. I hope you let him down easy."

"I think he's going to survive the breakup," she said wryly.

Gently, her brother asked, "And you?"

"Antonio? Never heard of him."

"That's the spirit."

"So about tomorrow night. Will it just be the three of us?" To her brother, she was giving nothing away. Not at this point, anyway. She would trust Caleb with her life. But this attraction to Rogan, well, it was too new to go broadcasting it to the whole family.

Caleb told her what she'd been longing to hear. "Rogan will be here, too. He's staying with us. You know, your dad's potential buyer? He says he met you today."

"Oh, yes. Rogan," she replied in a purposely neutral tone. *Did he say anything about me?* she longed to ask. But she didn't. "I liked him."

"He liked you, too. He says you're charming. And gorgeous."

Her pulse sped up again and her heart seemed to expand inside her chest, a sensation that somehow contained equal parts pain and pleasure. "Those Irish. Always with the flattery."

"Well, you *are* charming and gorgeous."

"I love absolute loyalty in a brother."

"I told him he was allowed to ask you out. But he'd better treat you right or he'd be dealing with me."

She groaned. "Oh, God. Caleb, you didn't."

He laughed. "Okay, I didn't. I only thought it."

She let out a relieved breath. "All right," she muttered grudgingly. "You get to live. What time tomorrow ight?"

"Seven?"

"See you then." She hung up in a very cool and collected manner.

And then she let out a whoop of excitement, jumped to her feet and set off at a wild run around the condo, from her office, to her bedroom, back down the hall, around the living room, dining room and kitchen area. She stopped at the counter by the sink, got down a glass, went to the water cooler and poured herself a drink, which she drained in one gulp, plunking the glass down hard when it was empty.

"Yes!" she shouted, loud and proud, not even caring that she was acting more like a preteen at a Jonas Brothers concert than a grown woman with a real job and a home of her own.

Rogan Murdoch thought she was charming and gorgeous.

And she would be seeing him tomorrow night—*and* Sunday, as well.

But first, there was lunch with her mother Saturday afternoon.

A year ago, Luz Cabrera had sold the beautiful Spanish-style house that Javier had built for the family. She'd moved into a smaller place near the office where she worked as a Realtor.

"What do I need with all this space?" she'd asked when she'd put the family home on the market. "It echoes of the life we knew, all of us, our family, together. That life is over. It's time I moved on."

They had lunch at the new house, out on the patio in the shade of a Mexican live oak. The house backed onto a golf course, so the view was of rolling greens and winding golf paths.

After the meal, they sat for a while, drinking iced te enjoying the welcome breeze.

Luz gathered her long dark hair off her neck and twisted it into a knot at the back of her head with a sigh. Elena studied her profile. Luz was fifty-two but looked younger. The last few years of heartache had aged her, though. The line of her jaw wasn't as firm as it had been. Her hair was still dark and vibrant as ever. But then, she had a great hairdresser who was genius with color.

Luz said, "I talked to your father last night. He wanted to tell me that he plans to sell the business to Caleb's friend."

Elena reached across the table and touched her mother's slim hand. "Does that upset you?"

Luz's dark brows drew together as she considered the question. Then she shook her head. "It's like the house, I think. Time to let it go." She eased her hand from under Elena's and clasped Elena's fingers. A quick, warm squeeze. "I think there is peace between us, at last."

"You and Dad?"

"Uh-huh. Did you know he went to counseling?"

That was a surprise. "No. He told you that?"

Luz nodded. "He said he had been wondering who he really was in all the trouble."

Elena didn't get that. "What do you mean, who he was?"

"A wronged husband—or a dangerous and violent man."

Elena jumped to her dad's defense. "*Papi*'s not dangerous. And he's kind, a good man. You know he is."

"*M'hija*." Her mother's voice was so gentle. "He hit me the day he found out. Only once, but hard enough to draw blood."

"I remember." At the time, she'd been so furious with her mother, she hadn't really stopped to consider that her father had actually struck her mom. She hadn't let herself admit how wrong that was. "He shouldn't have done that," she muttered, feeling a little ashamed of herself. And then she bit her lip and said no more. Anything else she said right then would probably be out of line.

Luz continued, "And he went after Davis with a gun. Remember that?"

Javier had fired that gun, too. The shot had grazed Aleta Bravo's arm when she jumped in front of her husband to protect him.

Elena bit her lip again. "Aleta forgave Dad for that. She understood what he was going through."

"But, *m'hija*, he needed to forgive *himself*. He needed to…understand himself better. He needed to face the wrongs he'd done, to make amends, so he could move on. We all need to do that when we hurt other people."

Elena wasn't sure what she felt at that moment. Anger, certainly. Yes, her father had done wrong. But her mom was no innocent in the whole thing.

Plus, Elena had become accustomed to the idea that her parents were finished. Yet now, the way her mother was talking, she was starting to wonder if there might be hope for their marriage, after all.

It had hurt so much to let hope go. She didn't know if she could bear to start hoping again. It was very confusing.

She asked, "So has Dad made amends to you, then?"

"Yes. He apologized to me, for hitting me. And for the more distant past, for the way he drove me away when we were young, for the part he played all those years ago in our early troubles. I accepted his apology. And also he's been to see Aleta, to make amends with her face-to-face. And with Davis, too."

Elena saw red. "Dad owes nothing to that man."

"Javier felt that he did. I agree with him. And your father

told me that Davis had a few amends of his own to make, that the two of them had a good talk."

"Why didn't anyone tell me about this?"

"*I'm* telling you. Now. And if you ask your father about it, I know he will be relieved to have it out in the open with you."

"And what about you, *Mami?*" Elena couldn't hold the question back. "Don't you need to make amends?"

Luz leaned back in the patio chair and rested her elbows on the chair arms, linking her hands across her lap. Her engagement diamond caught the light and glittered in a ray of sun that had slipped through the dappled shade of the oak that sheltered them. Luz had never taken off her rings.

"Yes," Luz said. "I need to make amends. Very much so. And I have done that, to the best of my ability. I have apologized to your father, for my betrayal of our marriage and our love, and for my many lies. I have also done my best to make amends to Aleta Bravo. I have prayed and taken confession and done the penance Father Joseph assigned me. And now, I live every day honestly. I tell the truth and I am straightforward with those I love." Luz spoke from the heart. Elena started to feel a little guilty for getting on her. But then Luz added, "And you're angry with me. Mercy said you would be."

"Mercy?" Fresh irritation made her voice sharp. "You already told her about all this?"

"Yes. She called this morning. We talked about it."

"Suddenly I feel like the baby of the family again. Always the last to know about everything that happens."

"Elena, *por favor.* I've told you both. And I only told your sister first because I talked to her before I talked to you."

Shamed, Elena dropped her gaze. "Sorry. I guess I'm kind of *acting* like the baby of the family...."

"It's okay," her mother said. "I understand. None of this is easy. There is so much pain. It's a natural thing to want to lash out when we are hurting."

Elena lifted her head, met her mother's loving eyes, and asked the big question. "So…does this mean you and Dad are considering getting back together?"

Slowly, Luz shook her head. "No. That part of our marriage is over. We live apart now and we are both accustomed to it. We both have a kind of peace now, of contentment."

A moment ago, Elena had been angry at the thought that they might reunite. Now, she ached at the idea that they never would. "What kind of marriage is it, if you don't even get to be together? Aleta and Davis worked it out, even though she moved out of their house and he had to crawl on his belly like the snake he is to get her back."

"Davis Bravo is not a snake," her mother said sternly.

Elena folded her arms across her chest, muttered, "Tell that to someone who cares," and knew that she was acting like a baby again.

Her mother made a low, sympathetic sound. And then lectured Elena some more. "Davis has made mistakes, yes. Big ones. As we all have. And now, what we want, all of us, is peace in the family. Because we are all one family now, united by *you, m'hija.* And by Mercy and Luke and Lucas and the new baby that's coming. United by your close bond with Caleb, your brother. *Una familia.* The Cabreras and the Bravos. You know that we are."

Elena did know. But they—her sister, her mother, all of them—asked too much of her. "Do not tell me that I have to make peace with Davis Bravo. I get enough of that from Mercy."

Her mother reached out again. She got hold of Elena's right wrist and tugged. Elena gave in and relaxed a little, letting her arms fall away from her chest, allowing her mother to take her hand.

Luz said, "I am not telling you what to do. You have to make your own decisions about your relationship with Davis."

Gently now, Elena pulled her hand free. She picked up her glass, sipped her tea. "There *is* no relationship between me and Davis."

Luz sank back to her own chair again. She stared at the tall glass of tea in front of her, but didn't reach for it. "I have told you what I needed to tell you. Why don't we speak of something more pleasant now?"

More pleasant. Like Rogan Murdoch.

But no. She wasn't ready to talk about him with anyone but her sister. And anyway, what was there to say? *About that guy who's buying dad's company? He told Caleb he thought I was charming and gorgeous. I really wish he would ask me out.*

Uh-uh. Either he would or he wouldn't. If it ever went anywhere with him, then she would have something to say to her mother about it.

She put on a smile. "I'm going to Bravo Ridge for Easter dinner tomorrow. Mercy talked me into it. How about you?" Mercy always invited their mom to the Bravo family dinners—and she invited their dad, too, though Javier never went.

"I don't think so," Luz said. Her eyes were full of memories.

When Elena and Mercy were young, Easter was a big day for the family. They all went to mass and took communion together, early in the morning. And, then, at home, when Elena was small, she hunted Easter eggs like any other American child. But by the time she was eight or nine, egg hunts were for babies. By then, Mercy was part of the family, too.

And in those years, they would often drive down to Corpus Christi and spend the day at the beach. Always, they had wonderful food. Avocado soup. Roast lamb to celebrate the end of Lent. *Agua de melón*. And *capirotada*, Mexican bread pudding, for dessert.

They were all together then, a happy family. And that was what mattered, that was what made Easter such a special day.

"I wish you would come, Mom," Elena said.

"Not this year."

They sat in silence for a while, sipping their tea, watching a golf cart roll along a winding trail until it disappeared in a stand of trees.

Her mother spoke again. "Forgiveness, *m'hija*. Sometimes I think it is the secret to a full life. We forgive and we let go. And then we can move on, we are ready to accept all the good that life still has to offer us, because we've made an open space in our hearts where bitterness and anger and our own secret guilts once lived."

"Mom. I promise you. I have no secret guilts."

"But anger and bitterness, eh? Maybe a little of those?"

"I thought we were moving on to more pleasant subjects, remember?"

"Ah, but to me forgiveness *is* pleasant. Better than pleasant. Forgiveness is the way to happiness."

Anticipation.

There was no other word for what Rogan was feeling.

He'd been looking forward to seeing Elena again since he'd sat across from her at lunch the day before. It was not a feeling he should have allowed himself, given that he'd already decided he would not ask her out.

She arrived at seven. He and Caleb were in the kitchen with Irina, keeping her company while she finished getting the meal ready. The doorbell rang and Rogan had to hold himself in check against the powerful urge to jump from the counter stool and run to get it.

"That's Elena." Caleb left them and returned a minute later, laughing at something his sister had said, carrying a bag of chips and a covered bowl.

Elena was right behind him. She looked as beautiful as she had the day before. Maybe more so. She wore a white strapless sundress printed with vivid red, pink and purple flowers. Her hair was down, thick and shining. And the velvet skin of her shoulders made him ache to touch her.

He wouldn't, of course. Not ever.

But hey. A man could dream.

"Hi," she said, sending him a bright smile that made weird things happen in the pit of his stomach.

"Hi, Elena."

She set the bottle of wine she'd brought on the counter and went over to greet Irina with a quick kiss on the cheek. "What are we having?"

"Cedar plank salmon, sweet and sour rice and roasted asparagus," Irina said in her throaty, slightly accented English.

"Yum. I brought white bean dip and olives for an appetizer."

"Perfect," Irina declared.

Elena took the bowl from Caleb and unwrapped it. It was the divided kind—olives on one side, dip on the other. Irina handed her a big basket for the chips.

For while, they all just stood around, chatting. Again, like yesterday at the restaurant, Rogan found it hard not to stare at Elena. That dimple at the corner of her mouth enchanted him. And he loved the husky sound of her laughter.

Eventually, they sat down to eat. Caleb got the salmon from out on the grill and opened the white wine Elena had brought. He poured for all but Irina, who was expecting their first baby in August. The food was great, the conversation easy.

Elena talked a little about her job teaching social studies to eighth graders, and Irina bragged about some deal Caleb had just made for BravoCorp, selling imported wine to a chain of high-priced restaurants.

Rogan talked about Murdoch Homes and his plans for expansion. Nobody mentioned Cabrera Construction, or the negotiations Rogan and Javier were deep into. That was fine with Rogan. It wasn't a done deal. Not yet, anyway.

The evening went by much too quickly. They finished the meal and sipped the last of the wine. Irina served dessert and coffee outside on the patio, poolside.

At ten, Elena got up to go.

Too soon.

Magically, Rogan found himself on his feet when she rose from her chair. Which was fine. The polite thing to do. After that, he meant to tell her it was nice seeing her again and then to sit back down.

But then he heard himself saying, "I'll walk you out...."

Caleb sent him a knowing look, which Rogan ignored. He turned and followed Elena inside. They went through the kitchen and on out to the front foyer.

It was a great place to be, following Elena. He watched the gentle swaying of her hips beneath the full skirt of her dress.

She turned to him at the door. He looked down into those

bronze-colored eyes of hers and felt dazed and confused and way too eager.

To kiss her.

To stay up all night talking with her. He didn't care in the least about what.

She said, "I'll see you tomorrow, I'm guessing—at the Bravo family ranch?"

He could get lost in the sound of her voice, in the tempting way her mouth moved when she talked.

"Rogan?"

He realized he'd been staring. And he hadn't answered her question. "Right. Easter dinner. I'll be there."

A smile played at the corner of her red lips and that dimple teased him, appearing, then vanishing. Then appearing again. "If you buy my father's business…" She let the sentence trail off.

He was lost in her eyes. And this close, the scent of her was driving him crazy. She smelled like a tropical garden. Jasmine and sandalwood. Gardenias. Orange blossoms.

Somehow, impossibly, he remembered to speak. "If I buy your dad's business, then what?"

"Will you be moving to San Antonio?"

He longed to nod, to lie outright, to tell her he was, yes. Absolutely. If she was here, he wanted to be here, too.

Absurd. Pointless. Over the top. Completely unlike him.

"No," he said. "I'll stay at the home office. One of my top contractors is willing to make the move, though. His name's Ellis Pierce. He's a good man, with a wife and two little girls."

"A wife and two little girls," she echoed. Her eyes shimmered with sudden tears. "Just like my dad, way back when."

"Right. I hadn't realized." And the last thing he'd meant to do was to make her cry. "Hey…"

She blinked, put on a tight smile and hitched her chin a fraction higher. "Hmm?"

"I'm sorry. What did I say?"

"It's not you, Rogan. Really." She glanced down, dark lashes like fans of silk against her cheeks. When she looked at him again, she had her tears under control. "Just sentimental, I guess. It's hard to picture my dad retired. Next thing you know, he'll be buying a Winnebago, heading for Florida or Arizona, where all the retired people go."

He wanted to comfort her. It was like a physical need in him—to pull her close to him, to guide her shining head down to rest on his shoulder.

But of course, he did no such thing. "Would that be so bad, your dad moving to Florida?"

"No. Not at all. As long as he's happy there—and what's that they say? 'The only constant in life is change.'"

"Ain't that the truth—but at this point, I feel obliged to add that nothing's settled yet. Your dad and I are still hammering out a deal."

"Ah. I see. The good man with the wife and the two little girls will be taking over *if* you and my dad work things out."

"Exactly. If…"

"You're being way too cautious, I think. I have a really strong feeling it's all going to work out." She gazed up at him with open invitation in those golden-brown eyes, clearly talking about more than his negotiations with Cabrera Construction. It was a very tempting offer. He ached to take her up on it.

Talk about playing with fire. He was smarter than that— or so he kept trying to tell himself.

She said, "You mentioned that your brother was your business manager?"

"Cormac. Yes." He braced a hand on the doorframe a few inches from her head, much too close to all that glorious gold-shot dark hair.

"Will Cormac be coming down here soon—I mean, *if* the negotiations continue?"

"Yes, he will. Next week."

"And you'll both stay here, at Caleb's?"

"No, we have a suite reserved at the Hilton—the one on the River Walk? Caleb and Irina have been great, but I don't want to take advantage of them."

"They have plenty of room. I think they'd love to have you *and* Cormac stay with them."

"That's what they said, too. But no. The Hilton will be perfect."

"So...the negotiations are moving right along, then?"

"Absolutely."

She slanted him a knowing look. "But you still won't admit that it's a done deal."

"Not yet."

"I'll look forward to meeting Cormac." She smiled—and there it was, that tempting dimple teasing him again, right there beside her way-too-kissable mouth.

It was his turn to say something. Anything. It didn't really matter what the words were, he realized. Only that he spoke. And she answered. "I like your dad."

"He likes you." Her gaze slid to his mouth—and then swiftly lifted again so she was looking in his eyes.

A kiss, he was thinking. Just one. How wrong could it be to steal one little kiss?

True, it couldn't go anywhere between them. But not everything had to go somewhere. It was such a simple, perfect moment. A beautiful woman, a whispered good-night.

A kiss. One kiss...

He went for it, stepping in a little closer, lowering his head.

She lifted hers.

Their lips met. Electric and tender.

He wanted to linger, to take her by the shoulders, pull her body close to his, to wrap his arms good and tight around her, to taste her more deeply.

To take his sweet time about it.

But he didn't. That wouldn't be right.

He lifted his head, whispered her name. "Elena..." It tasted so good in his mouth, as good as her lips had felt pressed to his, as good as the scent of her, sultry and sweet.

"Good night, Rogan." She slipped away from him, opened the door and went out.

He followed, as if pulled by invisible strings, and stood on the porch to watch her run down the walk away from him, the high heels of her red sandals tapping briskly with each step. At her car, she circled around to the driver's door, pausing when she got there to give him a last wave.

He lifted his hand, returned the gesture.

And then she was ducking inside. The engine started up. The car pulled away from the curb and rolled off down the street.

Rogan stood there on the front step after she was gone, thinking that he shouldn't have kissed her.

Wishing he had kissed her again.

Chapter Three

That night, Elena dreamed of Rogan. Of kissing Rogan. Of being with him in some hazy, romantic place where they talked about everything, all through the night.

But when she woke in the morning, she couldn't remember a single thing they'd said. All she knew was that she would see him again that afternoon.

She could not wait.

Eager for the day to come, she threw back the covers and headed for the shower. An hour later, she met her mother at church and they attended early mass together, took communion side-by-side. After mass, Elena suggested they share Easter breakfast.

But Luz only hugged her and said, "Not today, *m'hija.* Have a beautiful holiday...."

Elena almost told her then. *I plan to. Mami, I've met someone. Someone so special...*

But she didn't. She hugged Luz a second time and they parted on the church steps.

At home, she made coffee and stared out the kitchen window while it brewed, thinking about Rogan, trying to make the all-important decision as to what to wear to Bravo Ridge that afternoon. The knock came at the front door as she was filling a cup.

She went to answer and found her dad, wearing a white dress shirt and dark trousers, holding a bakery box. "I stopped in at El Mercado."

Laughing with pleasure at the sight of him, she took his arm and pulled him inside. "Just in time. I have the coffee ready."

She filled two cups, got out the milk and sugar and they sat at her kitchen table and ate *cuernos de azúcar*— Mexican croissants dusted with sugar—and lemon-filled empanadas.

"More coffee?" she asked.

At his nod, she got up and poured them both another cup and then carried the pot back to the warming ring.

When she returned to the table and slid into her seat, he reached out and laid his hand on her arm. "Elena…" All at once, his eyes were so serious, the set of his mouth way too grim.

A panicked tightness squeezed her throat. She gulped. "What is it? What's wrong?"

He patted her arm. "Please. Don't be afraid. It's nothing so terrible." A sad laugh escaped him. He withdrew his hand. "Or at least, it's nothing you don't already know about."

She remembered her mother's refusal to have breakfast with her. *Not today, m'hija*, Luz had said, but nothing about why not. "Mom knows you're here?"

He gave a slow nod. "She told me that she spoke with

you, about the ways we are working to have peace in our family, at last." He looked so uncomfortable. She ached for him.

"Dad, we don't have to talk about this."

"Ah. But I think we do. I want you to understand...." He seemed unsure how to continue.

She made a sound of encouragement. "What? Tell me."

He sipped from his cup, set it down with a tired sigh. "Most of the time I was a good husband to your mother. But not always."

"Yes. I know. It was bad, that you hit her."

"It was worse than bad. It was not acceptable. She betrayed me. She lied to me. And that hurt me deeply. But striking her was no answer to my pain. She had never—ever—done any violence to me."

Softly, she confessed, "*Mami* said you've been seeing a counselor."

He nodded again. "To try to...understand myself a little better, to face all the ways I have lied to myself over the years. To look honestly into my own heart, to face the darkness there."

An outraged sound escaped her and tears stung her eyes. "Darkness? What are you talking about? Why do you have to make yourself the bad guy in this? You're not. No way."

"Elena," he said so gently. "*No llores*. Don't cry..." He touched her arm again.

She grabbed for his hand, held it tight between both of hers. "Sorry." She sniffed, blinked away the moisture. "So sorry..."

"There is nothing for you to be sorry about. Know that. Believe that."

She nodded eagerly, clutched his hand tighter. "Yes. I

do. I know it. But I seem to have…oh, I don't know, a lot of heat on this whole subject, I guess you could say."

"It's not surprising. What happened has hurt you. *I* hurt you, by turning my back on you when I first learned that you weren't my blood child."

"That's all in the past. We got through it. It doesn't matter anymore."

Javier insisted, "It does matter."

"*Papi.* I understood. I really did."

He said nothing for a moment. Then he sighed. "You *are* my daughter," he said. "In all the ways that really matter."

She knew it already. Still, it felt so good to hear him say it out loud. She bit her lip, swallowed back a fresh flood of tears and leaned across the distance between them to press a kiss on his lined cheek.

He touched the side of her face, a tender caress. "You still blame your mother."

She sank back to her own chair, wanting to argue. But no. He was right.

He said, "You don't know how I was, how angry and bitter, when she went to work for Davis Bravo. No, she shouldn't have done what she did in betraying our marriage vows—and with my sworn, lifelong enemy, too. But I do see my part in it now. In some ways, time and growing older can be a man's best friend. He learns to see more clearly. And I see that I drove her away. I was angry, so angry—at the Bravos, for taking our land, taking everything. For the death of my father, which I blamed on James Bravo, though it was my father who broke into the Bravo ranch house with murder on his mind. It's not so hard now, to see that James Bravo had to protect himself and his family when he killed my father.

"And even more than for my father's death, I was angry

for...selfish reasons. For my idea of myself, as a man. I was angry because your mother and I had no babies, while my enemy had so many. I never hit your mother then, all those years ago. But I was cruel to her. I said hard things, things that hurt her. I called her barren. I said she was...no good, as a woman. I didn't want to face that the problem might lie with me...."

Elena's hand shook as she picked up her cup and took a slow sip. She knew he wasn't finished.

He went on, "And then she took that job working for Davis. I left her then. And Davis was kind to her. And he had his own problems at the time, he and Aleta. They...took comfort in each other, your mother and Davis. And both of them regretted what they did as soon as they had done it. Your mother left that job with him and she and I reunited. I was the happiest man alive the day she told me that she was going to have a baby—have *you*. And *we* were happy. So happy. Together."

Elena longed to argue that it wasn't right. It was all based on a lie. But what good would that do? Her mother's lie had been found out in time. In the end, they had all paid the price for it.

She turned away as she muttered bleakly, "Mom says you and Davis have made peace with each other."

"We have, yes," her father said. "We will never be friends. But I think we understand each other now. There can be true peace between us now. After all, we share two daughters...."

She took his meaning. Mercy was Davis's daughter-in-law. And she, Elena, was his...

Not his daughter. No. She refused to even let herself think it. "Next, you'll be telling me you want me to get to know him better." Her voice was tinged with bitterness and she felt only slightly bad about that.

Her dad just smiled. "No. I will give you no advice when it comes to Davis Bravo."

"Whew. Thank you."

"But I will say that if you decide you want to meet with him, to talk with him, to find your way to some kind of closeness with him, I will be pleased for you."

She gazed at him, disbelieving. "You're not serious."

"Ah, but I am. I told you, I see things much more clearly now. Don't deny your blood father for my sake. There is no law that says you can't have *two* fathers. The fact is you do have two fathers." She opened her mouth to deny it, but he stopped her words with a look. "I'm not telling you what to do, *m'hija*. I'm only saying, if you hold back from knowing Davis, let it be by your own choice. Don't lay the blame on me." He picked up his coffee and took a thoughtful sip.

She was thinking about her mom again. "You know, it's true what you said a few minutes ago. I love Mom. But I do blame her the most, I think, for everything that happened. She cheated and she lied. She lied every day for over twenty years."

"*M'hija*." With care, her father set down his cup. "Your mother knew me. She knew me so well. If she had told me the truth all those years ago, that she had been with Davis, that the baby—that *you* were Davis's blood and not mine… my anger was so deep then. You can't know how deep. I would have hurt her. And I would have gone after Davis. I might have killed him then, or someone close to him."

"No!" She didn't believe that.

He met her gaze steadily. "Yes," he said. "Yes. Consider what did happen three years ago. I hit your mother when I learned the truth. And I got my pistol and I went after Davis."

They were silent, the two of them, for what seemed like

a long time. Somewhere outside, she heard a woman, calling, "Jenny! Jenny, where are you?" And a child answered, "Here, Mommy! Coming…"

Her father said, "So instead of the truth when you were born, we had happiness. As a family. We grew prosperous. And when the truth finally found us, well, at least I was older, a little bit wiser. A little more able to learn, slowly, from the hard lessons life has thrown at me—at all of us. Can you see that?"

"Yes. All right. I…I see what you mean."

Her father almost smiled. "You're wondering why I've said all this, wondering why I thought you needed to hear it."

It had meant a lot—so very much—to hear him say out loud that she was his true daughter, to know that their bond was as strong as it had ever been. But as for the rest of it, well, "Maybe it was something you needed to tell me."

He chuckled then. "*Es verdad*. I did need to tell you." He was shaking his head. "I am so glad that I'm no longer young. It wasn't easy to be young. So much passion. So much frustration. And confusion. It's an exhausting time of life."

She reached for him again, caught his hand. "Are you okay, *Papi*? I mean, really okay? You look so tired."

He stood, pulled her close and wrapped her in a loving hug. "I *am* tired, yes. And yet, more myself. More…content than I have ever been."

She moved back enough to meet his eyes, but remained in the circle of his strong arms. "Content." She resisted the urge to make a sour face. "It's what Mom said."

"And we are content, your mother and I, both of us. Just as we are now. More than you know."

What could she say to that? No, she didn't get it. Didn't get how anyone could be satisfied with mere contentment.

Was that because she was still young, as he said, still young and full of passion and confusion? Whatever. If he was happy with being "content," well, who was she to argue with that?

Still, she couldn't help teasing him, "So maybe you and Mom should get back together. She could retire, too. You could travel a little, get out and see the world, be 'content' together."

He answered pretty much as her mother had. "I don't think so, *m'hija*."

She left it at that. In the end, it was her parents' business, whether they lived apart or not. She might be young, but she knew that much.

He left a few minutes later. At the door, he hugged her one more time and told her how much he loved her.

And when he was gone, she felt really good—lighter, somehow. As if the things her father had said had lifted a weight off her shoulders, a weight she hadn't even realized she was carrying. It occurred to her that this could end up being the best Easter ever, even if her mom and dad were apart.

At least there was peace between her parents now—what the psychologists always called "closure." They each had their own personal "contentment." Maybe that was as good as it got for them.

But not for her. She had her whole life ahead of her. Closure and contentment were the last things she wanted now.

She wanted excitement. Passion. Love, eventually.

And then everything that came with love: Commitment. Children. A family of her own.

But right now, what she wanted more than anything was to see Rogan Murdoch again.

And in a few hours, she would.

* * *

Rogan was beyond pissed at himself.

And he had been since about ten minutes after Elena drove away the night before, once he could no longer smell the tempting scent of her perfume. Once he'd returned to his senses.

What was the matter with him, to go leading her on like that? Walking her to the door. Flirting with her outright. *Kissing* her. He had more sense than that.

A man didn't make moves on a woman like Elena without knowing exactly what kind of signal he was giving her.

It had been wrong, what he'd done. That one amazing, unforgettable kiss would have been more than enough to get her thinking they were going somewhere with each other—at the very least, on a first date.

He thought about that. About how maybe he should ask her out. And then he could explain his situation. He could tell her frankly that if she wanted anything more than his company or maybe a hot night of good sex—or two—he wasn't her guy.

But considering his behavior last night, going out with her seemed like just begging for trouble. If he couldn't keep his hands off her when they were at Caleb's, with her adoring and protective big brother nearby, how was he going to exercise restraint if it were just the two of them?

No.

A date was not the answer.

Avoidance was. She was going to think he was a jerk, and he deserved that. Really, if you got right down to it, he *was* a jerk for sending her signals when he had no intention of following through on them.

Rogan went to the Bravo ranch determined to stay as far away from Elena Cabrera as he possibly could.

* * *

That plan lasted about an hour.

Until he saw her again. She walked in the front door of the big Bravo ranch house and he was a goner.

Was it possible she could be even more gorgeous that day than the night before? She wore a close-fitting white-dotted dark blue dress and a short-sleeved white jacket. She had her hair swept up, soft little curls escaping to kiss the back of her slim golden neck. He wished he was one of those little curls so he could brush against that neck.

It was hopeless. Really. No way could he resist her.

He hung back as she hugged her sister and exchanged greetings with Caleb, and then he moved in.

She turned and smiled at him, dimple flashing. Pure temptation. "Rogan." She laughed and the sound was as fine as the scent of her. "It's been so long."

"Hours," he said. It came out in a growl.

Ridiculous. Insane. Totally unacceptable.

He only wanted to be near her. Was that so damn wrong?

He knew it was.

Still, wrong or not, he stayed near her.

First, they wandered into the kitchen together and chatted with Mercy and Aleta and a couple of the other Bravo wives.

And an hour later, there was an egg hunt out on the back grounds for the kids. Only a few of them were the right age for it, but they seemed to have a ball. Their parents followed them around and everyone else got comfortable on patio furniture arranged around the pool and on the edges of the lawn.

Rogan and Elena found chairs side by side and watched the kids racing all around in the grass, under the oak trees and even along the pretty trails of the formal garden, doting parents following after them. Lucas—Mercy and Luke's toddler—was especially cute. He was in too much of a hurry for his fat little legs and he kept falling over into the grass. But falling didn't stop him. He would struggle upright again, grab his basket and lurch off in a different direction, laughing the whole time.

Besides Lucas, there was seven-year-old Kira, Matt and Corrine Bravo's older girl, and three-year-old Ginny, Mary Bravo's daughter from her first marriage.

As Rogan watched, Lucas took another header onto the grass. His big cousin Kira, who happened to be a few feet away, darted over to help him up.

"Lucas," she scolded. "You have to be more *careful*."

"Kira, no!" he commanded, batting her hands away. "I do it, me."

"Oh, fine. You just go ahead." Kira made a disgusted sound and whirled away, the full skirt of her pink Easter dress belling out around her.

"Kira is the greatest kid." Elena leaned close to him, bringing a sweet hint of jasmine that made his head swim. "But also really bossy. Sometimes she reminds me of Mercy."

He turned his head to meet those brandy-colored eyes. "Mercy was a bossy big sister?"

"Oh, yeah. She and her mom didn't come to stay with us until she was eleven—did Caleb tell you my parents adopted her after her mom died?"

"He did mention that, as a matter of fact."

A frown creased her smooth brow. "Really? What *else* did he mention?"

"He explained all the…complicated family relation-
ships—in a very general way."

She rolled those amazing eyes. "Well. If you know that

Caleb's my half brother, it's not that hard to put it together, anyway, I guess."

Settling back into her chair, she stared out across the lawn again, toward where Davis and Aleta sat together, holding hands, beaming like the proud grandparents they were. "They've been married for about thirty-five years." Her voice was flat. "I'm twenty-five. One of them cheated. It wasn't Aleta."

He leaned closer to her again and she turned to meet his gaze. Her eyes were stormy now, her mouth set. "You're angry," he said. "Maybe we should change the subject."

"I'm not angry. But suit yourself."

He wanted to touch her, soothe her. But he kept his hands to himself. "Look. It's okay. If talking about your relationship with Davis makes you uncomfortable, I get it. And I'm more than ready to move on."

She sighed, a tender little sound, and the thick fans of her eyelashes swept down. After a long moment, she looked at him again, the hostility gone now. "Sorry. I don't mind talking about it. I'm not happy with the whole situation, but everyone tells me I need to get over that."

"But you're not—over it, I mean."

"No. I guess I'm not." She didn't elaborate.

He didn't push. "And you were saying, about Mercy being bossy...?"

Instantly, her expression brightened. "Oh. Right. She started bossing me around the first day she moved in with us. A natural big sister. I resented her totally. And I also completely adored and idolized her."

"Sounds like the perfect big sister to me."

"She was. She is." Her mouth was so soft. He remembered how good it had felt, kissing her. He wanted to do again. Right there, on the back grounds of the Bravo ra⁻ house, during the family egg hunt.

Somehow, he managed not to.

But it was a near thing.

Little Ginny, in a lavender dress with a big satin bow, had just found another egg. She bent at the waist, the wide hem of her dress lifting out behind her. Grabbing the egg, she straightened and held it high. "I got one, I got one!"

Rogan chuckled at the sight.

Elena was watching him. "You like kids?"

"I'd better. I just finished raising three of them."

"Does this remind you of the egg hunts of your childhood?"

"Yeah. Mostly the later ones, when I was too big for hunting eggs and got to help my parents hide them. I felt so grown-up, I remember, watching my sister and brothers running around the backyard, letting out little squeals of triumph each time one of them found another egg."

She chuckled. "I always wanted a big brother." Her expression changed, grew thoughtful. "And now I have seven of them." She tipped her chin up, cheerful and defiant at the same time. "So I guess being Davis Bravo's love child isn't *all* bad."

He thought she looked a little bit lost, suddenly. And the need to touch her got the better of him. He reached for her hand, twined his fingers between her slim, soft ones. "Don't be sad," he whispered. "Think of Caleb. Can you imagine your life now without Caleb? I know he couldn't get along without you."

She almost smiled. "Yeah. It's funny. We grew close really fast, right after we found out the truth. And you're right. It's like he's always been my brother, somehow..."

The brother in question was sitting with Irina a few feet away. Were his ears burning? Maybe. When they both turned to look at him, Caleb stared back, one eyebrow lifted.

And Rogan was still holding Elena's hand.

Seriously, he needed to get a grip. What about all those promises he'd made himself, the ones about how he would stay the hell away from her?

And yet here he was, his head bent close to hers, drinking in the scent of her, hanging on her every word, fingers woven with hers.

He should let go. But he didn't.

A couple of minutes later, she did it for him. Gently, she eased her hand away, a slight smile curving her beautiful mouth, a blush on her cheeks.

The egg hunt wound down. Then Luke suggested a walk out to the stables. He raised horses on the ranch.

The men agreed to go with him, and the women, taking the children, headed for the kitchen to start pulling the meal together. Rogan gathered what little sanity remained to him and went with the men.

But later, at dinnertime, he caught up with Elena again. They sat together. He took great care not to touch her, not even in passing, not to lean too close. Somehow, he succeeded in getting through the meal without putting his hands on her.

After dinner, everyone helped clear the table. They took a break before dessert. Some wandered into the big living room, some of them chose the game room, which had a pool table and cabinets full of board games. Others went out in back again to sit by the pool or under the trees.

Elena stayed with Mercy, Mary Bravo and Irina in the kitchen. Rogan headed for the game room and played pool with Caleb for a while. Surprisingly, his friend said nothing about the way he'd been hanging all over Elena— sitting beside her at dinner and holding her hand during the egg hunt. Rogan was grateful for Caleb's silence on the subject. Again, he promised himself to show restraint from now on.

That promise lasted about an hour and a half. Until they all returned to the formal dining room for coffee, coconut cake and homemade ice cream.

Elena had saved a chair for him. What could he do but sit beside her, get lost in her eyes, drown in her laughter, become drunk on the scent of her skin?

After dessert, the two of them went into the living room together. They sat close on one of the long sofas there. By the time everyone started making time-to-go-home noises, he had more or less accepted that he really needed to stop lying to himself, stop making himself promises he was not going to keep.

He liked Elena. A lot. And she clearly liked him. She was twenty-five years old. All grown-up. If he wanted to be with her and she wanted to be with him, well, why not? There was no need to make a big deal out of something so simple.

If it went beyond this dizzying attraction, beyond friendship, well, he would be honest with her. He would tell her he wasn't up for anything permanent, that they could enjoy each other's company while he was in town.

And that would be it.

Then she could make her own choice about where to take it from there.

It all sounded very mature and logical. He congratulated himself on coming to such a realistic solution to the problem that had seemed so unworkable, but really wasn't.

However, by the time he accepted that he was going to ask her out, she had left him, promising to be right back. He had no idea where, exactly, she'd gone. And then Caleb came over and said they should be going soon.

Rogan really wanted to see her before they left—even

though it would be easy to get her number from Caleb and take it from there. He started toward the back of the house, thinking she might be in the kitchen with her sister. But in there, he found only the two women Mercy had hired to help with the party. They were busy cleaning up. He headed down the hallway toward the game room and the sun room farther on.

There were six doors lining that hallway, three on either side. Two on the left were side doors into the formal and family living areas. One on the right led to an office, one to a library. The last door on the left was shut. But the final door on the right was open.

And he heard Elena's voice from inside, the sound tight, strictly controlled. "This is not necessary. Really. I would prefer just to leave it alone."

"Elena. You're my daughter." A man's voice. Deep. Mature. Commanding. Rogan didn't need to be a psychic to know who that man was: Davis Bravo.

Chapter Four

The deep voice from inside the room continued, "I only hope to know you better. I care about your welfare, and your...happiness."

"Then there's no problem." Elena was making a valiant effort to keep it cool. Rogan could hear that effort in every strung-tight word she said. "Honestly. I'm doing well. I'm perfectly happy."

"Please," Davis said, "The trust is yours, no strings."

"No, thank you."

"It's there for you, no matter what. At least visit my estate planners, let them explain—"

"No. Please."

"All right. Never mind the money for now. But maybe we could try meeting for coffee, just the two of us, for an hour. Just to—"

"Look." She cut him off a second time. "I'll, um...

I'll think about it. Okay? And I really have to get going now."

"Elena…"

"No. It's enough. Seriously. I need to go. Bye now." She came flying out that door. And straight into Rogan's arms. "Oh!" She landed against his chest and gaped up at him. "Rogan!" She jumped back.

"Hey. Steady." He resisted the need to pull her close again.

She put her hand to her hair, smoothed the front of her dress. "What are you doing here?"

"We're getting ready to go. I wanted to say goodbye."

Right then, Davis emerged from the room behind her. He looked every bit as imposing as he sounded, a tall, broad-shouldered man with thick silver hair. He turned his ice-green eyes on Rogan. "Get an earful?" His tone made it painfully clear that it wasn't wise to mess with Davis Bravo.

Elena leapt to Rogan's defense, stepping close to him again. "He was just looking for me, Davis. It's not a big deal."

"I had a really good time today." Rogan offered his hand to the older man. "Thanks."

Apparently, Davis wanted Elena's goodwill more than he wanted to put Rogan in his place. He dropped the aggressive attitude. "Well, I'm glad." He took Rogan's hand, gave it a single firm shake. "But don't thank me. Thank Elena's sister. Mercy put it all together, with a little help from my wife."

"Well, it was great."

Davis granted him a regal nod before turning his cool green gaze on Elena again. "Consider what I said?"

"Yes," she answered reluctantly, not quite meeting his eyes. "All right."

Davis left them, striding back down the hall and disappearing through the door to the formal living room.

The moment he was out of sight, Rogan took Elena's hand. "Come on."

She hung back. "What? Where?"

"Hell if I know. Somewhere we can get a little privacy."

"Oh, Rogan…" But she let him pull her along back down the hall. He chose the office, which was more of a study, really, with a heavily carved mahogany desk and bookshelves lining the walls.

Once he pulled her in there, he swung the door shut and braced a hand against it.

She laughed. "Rogan, what are you up to now?"

"Are you okay?"

She looked at him sideways. "How much did you hear?"

He shrugged. "Enough. You have a trust fund you won't touch. And you don't want to meet your bio-dad for coffee."

She groaned. "My *bio*-dad? You make him sound like hazardous waste or something."

"Well, you have to admit, that's pretty much how you treat him."

She tried to look disapproving. "It's rude to eavesdrop on people."

"I know. I shouldn't have done it. If my mom were still alive, she'd be very disappointed in me."

"So why did you?"

Because I'm interested in you, way too interested. And that means I'm interested in anything that concerns you. "Have dinner with me. Tomorrow night?"

She didn't even pretend to think it over. "Yes." Her eyes gleamed golden in the light from the desk lamp. He wanted her. Bad. He wished he wasn't staying at Caleb's, wished he could take her somewhere tonight. Someplace where there was no possibility that they might be interrupted. She accused, "You didn't answer my question."

"Because I don't have an answer," he lied. "Other than that I was looking for you, heard you talking and got curious as to what was going on in there."

"It was none of your business."

"I plead guilty. And how about if I promise never to do it again?"

She folded her arms across her middle. "I don't know. Do you keep your promises?"

"Always." *Except for the ones I keep making to myself about staying away from you.*

She let her arms relax. "Well, all right then. As long as you never spy on me again, you're forgiven." She started to turn away, toward the desk.

He reached out, grabbed her hand again, and pulled her close to him. "Where do you think you're going?"

"To get a pencil and a piece of paper." She put both hands against his chest. They felt really good there. "You know, to write down my address and phone number?"

"In a minute."

"Rogan…" She said his name as a warning. But not a very convincing one. He touched her hair. Warm silk.

And then he went farther. He ran the back of his finger along her cheek. She felt as good as she looked. Maybe even better. And the way she watched him, with a sort of rapt expression, her eyes wide and willing, her mouth slightly parted…it was a look of pure invitation.

An invitation to a kiss.

He reminded himself to speak. "How about if I pick you up at seven?"

"Seven works."

He let his finger stray downward, to trace the clean, pure line of her jaw, and lower still. He caressed the side of her neck.

She swayed closer, caught herself, pulled back again, though she remained in the circle of his arms. "This is Luke's office," she whispered.

"Very nice." He was looking only at her. He lowered his head.

She tipped her head slightly, enough that he couldn't capture her mouth. "There is no kissing in Luke's office."

"Says who?"

She frowned. "Well, I don't know. Somehow, it just seems…inappropriate."

"Elena." He really liked the sound of her name and he couldn't get over the way it felt on his tongue, a gentle curving of sound. "Trust me. Luke won't mind."

She swayed a fraction closer again. "Well, if you're sure…"

"I have never been more certain about anything."

"Ah."

"Ah, what?"

"Ah, I suppose you'd better kiss me, after all." Her breath smelled so sweet, like apples flavored slightly with coffee and coconut.

He took her mouth. Gently. With slow deliberation, he rubbed his lips back and forth across hers in a light, teasing little kiss that nonetheless felt as though it was striking sparks.

"Be careful," she warned on a breath, her lips moving against his.

He caught her lower lip between his teeth, so lightly, touched the silky plumpness with his tongue. She shuddered a little, surrendering. Only then did he let go. "Careful of what?"

"Everything. Nothing. Oh, Rogan. I don't know...."

He settled his mouth more firmly on hers. Never mind about being careful. Never mind about anything.

There was nothing but this. Elena. Here. Now. Held close in his arms.

Closer. He wrapped his arms tighter around her.

She sighed and opened to him, tasting of flowers and coconut, of everything sweet.

And hot. And wet...

He eased his tongue inside, scraping it slowly along the edges of her teeth. She made a low, receptive sound.

He answered with a groan and ran his tongue over hers—over, around. And under.

When he retreated, she followed—a little shy, but definitely willing.

The scent of her intoxicated him and the feel of her made him forget all those promises he'd made, the ones about her, the ones he hadn't been keeping anyway. He could go on and on like this, his arms around her, her body warm and eager, her breasts so full and soft, pressed against him. He loved the feel of her hands on him—one curled around his nape, shyly ruffling his hair, the other on his shoulder, clutching him to her.

But then she put both hands against his chest again. She exerted a very slight pressure.

He got the message and lifted his head.

She gazed up at him, dreamy-eyed. "You make me feel..." She sighed. "So good."

He couldn't resist. He kissed her some more. He never wanted to stop.

But even drunk on her kisses, he didn't completely forget himself. They were at her family's ranch, in her half brother's study. And soon enough, Caleb would come looking for him.

It really was time to go.

With slow reluctance, he raised his head. "Tomorrow," he said, reminding himself as much as her. Tomorrow, after all, wasn't *that* far away. It only seemed like a lifetime when he thought how he wouldn't see her until then. Until hours and hours from now.

Seriously. He was getting way out of control about her.

Still holding his gaze, smiling a little, so that dimple of hers just barely tucked its tempting shadow into her cheek, she reached behind her, took both his wrists and peeled them away. She stepped back, turned and went to the desk.

Crossing around behind it, she pulled open the pencil drawer, took out a pen and wrote on the small notepad that sat waiting next to the computer monitor. She tore off the page, put the pen away and returned to him.

He held out his hand. She put the little square of paper in the center of his palm and closed his fingers over it. "Seven."

"Seven."

They stared at each other. Eventually, she advised, "You have to move away from the door now."

"I was afraid you would say that."

She let go of his hand and stepped back, giving him room to turn and pull open the door. He held it wide. She went through and on down the hall. He didn't follow. He waited until she turned for the kitchen, before he started for the door that led to the living room.

Caleb dropped in at Rogan's room after Irina went to bed. "Got a minute?"

Rogan sent off the last email and shut down his laptop. "Sure."

Caleb stayed in the doorway. "So you really like my sister, huh?"

"Yeah. I do."

"You ask her out?"

"I did. She said yes. Dinner, tomorrow night."

"Well, all right. Have a good time."

Rogan let out a grunt of laughter. "What? No overprotective big-brother lecture?"

"What's the point? You hurt her, you're dead. But I feel confident that you know that already." He glanced down at the floor and then up again. "Just kidding."

"Yeah. Right." Rogan considered telling his friend about the conversation he'd overheard between Elena and Davis. But no. If either of them wanted Caleb to know about it, they would tell him themselves. And maybe Caleb already did know.

As Elena had so clearly informed him, it was none of Rogan's business.

Now Caleb looked sheepish. "Don't tell her I said that—about your death, I mean. She would kick my ass for butting in."

"Don't worry. Your death threats can be our secret."

Caleb frowned. "Did I say I was kidding?"

"Yeah."

"Don't believe a word I say."

The phone was ringing when Elena let herself in the door of her condo. She went to the living room to get it. The display read: Mercy.

Of course.

She picked up and muttered, "What?"

"You sound surly."

"I am surly. What?"

"It was a big party." Mercy's voice was reproachful. "We didn't get a moment alone."

Elena held back a groan. "Sometimes that's not a bad thing."

"Davis said he talked to you. He said he really hopes you'll think about meeting him for lunch one of these days."

"Mercy, you're getting really overbearing about this. You know that, don't you?"

"I only want you to come to some sort of…peace with him."

"I'm at peace, okay?"

"Oh, you are not."

"And I really wish you'd quit discussing me with him."

"*Chica*, I'm on your side. I want the best for you. I want *everything* for you."

Elena thought of their father, of his visit that morning. Grudgingly, she told Mercy, "*Papi* came over this morning. We talked. About a lot of things." She filled her sister in on the confessions their dad had made.

"Wow," said Mercy when she was done. "*Papi*'s come a long way."

"Yeah. He really has. And he…gave me his blessing, if I want to, um, get to know Davis."

"That's good. Really good."

"And tonight I told Davis I would think about maybe having coffee with him sometime."

"Oh, Elena. I'm so glad."

"So can we leave it at that, leave whatever is or isn't going to happen between me and Davis…between me and Davis?"

"I only want for you to—"

"Mercedes, I know what you want. You've told me about thousand times. Please don't tell me again."

A silence, then, "Yeah. Okay. But if you need to talk about it—"

"You're the first one I'll come to. You know that."

"Good." Then, more softly, "I know I've been a real pain about this."

"No kidding."

"But the time goes by, you know? If you let too much of it get past you, well, you wake up one day and someone you should have made peace with is gone. You missed your chance. It's too late."

"I see that. I do." And Elena knew that her sister was talking about more than her and Davis. Mercy had barely known her own birth father. He'd died in a bar fight when she was very small. "And I also see that sometimes you never even get a chance to make peace with the ones who mean so much in your life."

"That's right. So when there is a chance—"

"I know, Mercy. When there is a chance, we really need to reach out and take it."

"I love you, *chica*." Her sister's voice was tender as a wound.

"And I love you."

For a sweet, full moment, they were silent together, a warm, close kind of silence, the silence you only know with the person you feel free to say anything to.

Then Mercy said, "Davis also mentioned that he caught Rogan Murdoch listening in on your private conversation."

Elena snapped to Rogan's defense. "He wasn't *listening in*—well, not exactly."

"And Davis said more."

"Oh, great. Worse?"

"Better. But if you don't want to hear it…"

"You are impossible. Seriously."

"Well, I just mean that if you—"

"*Díme*," Elena demanded. "Tell me."

"Oh, fine. Davis said he liked Rogan, said he respects a man who doesn't make a bunch of fake excuses for his bad behavior."

"Bad behavior. Well, I guess Davis ought to know."

"Elena. Be nice—and let me guess. Rogan asked you out."

"Yes, he did."

"I knew he would. He's obviously way interested."

Elena beamed at her own reflection in the decorative mirror over the mantel. "We're going out to dinner tomorrow night."

"Have a wonderful time."

"I will. No doubt about that."

Rogan arrived right on time.

And when she opened the door to him, his green gaze ran over her, taking everything in, making her feel so pretty. So feminine. He said he liked her silk dress, which was simple and sleeveless with a scoop neck. She invited him in, but he said they should get going. They had reservations.

He took her to a downtown steak house where the beef was prime and the wine list extensive. Rogan got them a private table in a corner nook. They had a really good Cabernet and took their time over appetizers, with filet mignon for the main course. And for dessert, they shared a serving of bread pudding with whiskey sauce.

They talked and talked. Hours went by and she hardly noticed the time passing. She asked how it had been, being a brother and a single parent at the same time.

He said, "At first, after our parents died, I didn't have a clue what I was doing. It was pretty grim."

"I can't even imagine."

"We were all in shock and Niall, the youngest of us three boys, started resenting me, that I would dare to try and take over our mom and dad's place. And Brenda? It seemed like she did nothing but cry and throw things for the first year or so. Cormac is more levelheaded. We always got along. He backed me up with the other two."

She laughed. "The way you say that. *The other two.* As if there should be ominous music in the background..."

He looked down into his wineglass, took a slow sip. "I guess I'm overplaying it a little."

She shook her head. "No. Really. I didn't say that. Don't for a minute think I'm minimizing what you went through."

"I don't." His gaze was warm. Appreciative. He said, "But really, Niall and Brenda weren't *that* bad. They just didn't appreciate having to do what their big brother told them to do. And they missed Mom and Dad. We all did. It was awful. A gaping, ragged hole in our lives where the center used to be, you know?"

"Oh, Rogan..." She reached across the white-clothed table, brushed his arm, an understanding touch.

He made a low noise in his throat. His eyes were far away now. "Niall is in law school, UT."

"UT. Just like his big brother."

"Niall wants to be a trial lawyer. It's a job I think he'll love because he never met a position he couldn't argue with—and if I sound cynical, I'm not. Brenda's the baby of the family and she acted like one. But Niall was the true rebel. With the tats and the piercings. At one point, it seemed like there wasn't anywhere on his face that didn't have a safety pin stuck in it. He hung out with druggies."

She shook her head. "You must have been scared to death for him."

"I was. But you know, he never got crossways with th

law. And all his tattoos are in places you can't see when he's wearing a button-down shirt. He had a couple of bad years, but then he seemed to get some focus. His grades improved. He got high SAT scores and had his choice of colleges. And now he's found what he wants to do with his life. So it's all good."

"I'm so glad. And Brenda?"

"She's gorgeous and smart. Not that I'm prejudiced."

She grinned at him. "Of course not."

"And she wants to be an actress. Between you, me and the wall, I can't understand why anyone would want to get up in front of a bunch of people and pretend to be someone else. Plus, it's not exactly a secure line of work. But it's her dream. And as her big-brother-slash-stand-in-parent, I figure it's my job to support her dream."

"Well said." She clinked her glass to his.

"Brenda's going to NYU in the fall."

"Wow. I know zip about theater programs. But even I've heard that NYU is a top theater school."

They were eating dessert by then. He scooped up a spoonful of bread pudding. "You go to UT?"

"Uh-uh. Berkeley."

"Whoa. That's a ways from Texas."

"I loved it. Getting out on my own, living in California in the Bay Area. Meeting lots of new people with interesting ideas…"

"Did you wear flowers in your hair and practice free love?"

"Rogan." She looked at him sideways.

He faked an innocent expression. "What did I say?"

"The flowers and the free love? That was like 1968."

"I know. But a guy can fantasize, can't he?"

"Well, I did go to Golden Gate Park once or twice.

And to a couple of rock concerts. And I found an ancient Make Love, Not War T-shirt at a street sale. I even wore it once."

"You would look great with flowers in your hair. A hibiscus, maybe, over one ear..."

"You think?" She couldn't resist him. She leaned in closer.

He mirrored her movement, capturing her hand, pressing his warm lips to the back of it and reaching out, guiding a swatch of her hair behind one ear. Her skin seemed to grow warmer wherever he touched her. And a shiver of anticipation trembled through her.

"A hibiscus," he said again. "Absolutely."

They stared into each other's eyes for a while. She thought how she really liked this mutual attraction thing. You could have the best time of your life just sitting at a table in a restaurant, looking at each other endlessly, smiling like a couple of borderline fools.

She thought of Tonio, suddenly, for some reason. Tonio and Tappy. She imagined them sitting together somewhere, holding hands just like her and Rogan, blissfully happy. The thought made her smile.

Rogan's mouth tipped up at the corners in response. "What?"

"Just hoping everybody in the world is happy tonight."

He touched her cheek again, so lightly, kind of cradling the side of her face. His palm was slightly rough and very warm. She felt like a cat, petted. Purring. "Are you happy, Elena?"

"Oh, yes. I am."

It was after eleven when they got back to her condo. He kissed her at her door, a lingering kiss.

And then she turned to fiddle with the lock as he waited close behind her. Thrillingly close.

He put those big, warm hands of his on her shoulders and a lovely sort of weakness overtook her. She instantly leaned back against him. He lowered his head, pressed his lips to the curve where her neck met her shoulder.

She sighed in pleasure, reached back to hold him there, sliding her fingers into his silky hair, forgetting all about getting the door open as his kiss trailed up the side of her neck, sparking delicious, exciting sensations. The keys dropped to the welcome mat and she could not have cared less as she turned in his arms and captured his mouth.

They shared a long, searing, perfect kiss.

"Come inside," she whispered at last against his mouth.

He pressed one more quick, hard kiss on her trembling mouth and then bent to scoop up the fallen keys. Handing them over, he stepped back that time, so she could open the door without any tempting distractions. Her hand trembled a little as she fit the key into the lock.

She ushered him in ahead of her, stopping in the small foyer to turn on another light and disarm the simple alarm. He went on, into the living room. She followed, switching on the lamp by the sofa and the torchiere lamp by the mantel.

He took in the rose-colored sofa and chairs, the sage green walls, the dark plank floor. "This is beautiful." And then he reached for her and kissed her again.

She'd been thinking she might offer coffee or a last drink. Or something.

But he didn't seem interested in anything but kissing her. And that was fine. She wasn't all that interested in anything else, either.

Somehow, they ended up on the sofa. And she was

breathless, transported. Her whole body shimmered with excitement and anticipation of what was to come.

Her first time. At last. Her first time—and with the perfect man.

He touched her bare upper arm, running his big, rough-palmed hand downward over her elbow, along her forearm. How could something so simple, one long, stroking touch, be so very sexual? So exactly right?

How could the feel of his lips against her skin make her whole body tremble, make her pull him closer, make her moan deep in her throat?

She kicked off her high-heeled shoes and leaned back on the couch arm. He bent over her, his mouth locked with hers, joined with her in a kiss that seared her to the core.

And then he touched her breast. Even through her dress and bra, that caress seemed to burn her—to set her on fire. She speared her hands up into his hair and dragged his mouth down. Lower.

Along the curve of her throat, which she arched for him, to the top of her chest. He kissed the bare flesh above the scoop neck of her dress, sending flares of need all through her, making her moan some more.

And she wanted...

Everything.

To be naked with him, to make love with him. To do everything a woman could do with a man. To be intimate with him in the most complete way.

At last.

She pressed a hand to his chest, loving the hardness and heat of him, wanting only to get rid of his shirt. And her dress. And everything, every last scrap of clothing that separated them.

And then he was rising, scooping her up with him a

he stood. She let out a surprised little laugh as she found herself high in his arms.

"The bedroom?" He kissed her as he said it.

She kissed him back and pointed the way.

Chapter Five

In her room, he eased her down until her feet met the rug at the side of the bed.

And then he kissed her some more. Endless, wet kisses. Kisses that made her only more certain that this was the night. And he was the right man.

She pressed herself so close to him, as they stood there, kissing by the bed. So close, she could feel him, feel his hardness, the proof of how much he wanted her. It felt... really good. Exciting.

Heedless of everything but this magic between them, she lifted her hips to him, rubbed herself shamelessly against him. It seemed so natural with him. So exactly what she ought to be doing with him.

But then his caressing hand found the tab of her zipper at the nape of her neck. He took that zipper down, the back of her dress falling open, baring her back.

And there seemed something so momentous about that.

about the first step to being fully undressed with him, that she broke the endless kiss they shared.

She held the front of the dress to keep it from falling off and she gazed up at him, watched his eyes go from lazy and hot, from deepest, darkest green, to a clearer color, one with questions in it.

He clasped her shoulders, gazed steadily down at her and she looked up at him. It was one of those looks, the kind she was already accustomed to sharing with him.

A speaking look.

He said, "We should talk, huh?"

She nodded.

He guided her around. She guessed what he would do and she smoothed her hair out of his way. He zipped her dress back up again. She reached behind her, caught his hand and turned again to perch on the edge of the bed, pulling him down so he sat beside her.

He raised her fingers to his lips. The feel of his mouth, the warm rush of his breath against her skin, thrilled her. Such a simple thing to get her whole body humming with desire all over again.

She said, "I don't know where to start."

"I have things to say, too." He sounded so calm. So sure. She wished she were half as relaxed about this as he seemed to be.

"Oh. Well, okay. Shall I, um, go first?"

He gave her an encouraging smile. "Go for it."

She cleared her throat, almost wishing she had left it alone, let nature take its course. Yes, it was important, to be responsible, to agree on birth control and all the other awkward stuff.

But still…

It was a lot more fun when he was kissing her senseless, lot easier just to let herself be swept deliciously away.

And why was it that now she'd made him stop kissing her, now she'd made it clear they needed to discuss all the ways they would be sexually responsible, she felt painfully shy, hopelessly inept?

She tried for a light touch. "The good news is I'm on the pill." She cringed as she said it. Not smooth, not in the least. And it seemed so lame, just to leave it at that. It seemed as if she should explain, somehow—and then, to her horror, she did start explaining. "I...had this boyfriend..." And as soon as she started, she couldn't seem to stop. "I thought that maybe we would...oh, well, you know. I hoped it would develop into something really good. Which was why I started on the pill. I kept thinking it would happen, between him and me. And somehow, the moment was never quite right and he and I never really went anywhere, as a couple, you know? I mean, I guess what I'm saying is it... didn't work out. And I..." All at once, she heard herself ask in a desperate whisper, "Oh, what am I doing?" She eased her hand free of his and covered her eyes. "Did I just say all that? Talk about too much information." She let out a groan. "Excuse me while I sink right through the floor."

"Hey." His voice was gentle, with just a hint of laughter in it. And then he was wrapping his warm fingers around her wrists, peeling her hands away from her eyes. And once he had her looking at him again, he cradled the side of her face. "Sometimes it doesn't work out. I know how that is."

"Oh, Rogan. Somehow, you always manage to say just the right thing." With a low groan, she swayed toward him. They kissed.

It was a good kiss, sweet and slow. Not deep, but still exciting. And also, somehow, wonderfully reassuring.

Eventually, though, the kiss ended. And again, they were two people who could sit in a restaurant together and ta' for hours, two people who were seriously attracted to each other—and yet, still, didn't know each other all that well.

Right then, at that moment, she was very much aware that they were hardly more than strangers when you got right down to it.

He asked, "Anything else?"

"Yes." She really did feel she had to tell him, that it wouldn't be right just to let him find out for himself.

"Tell me."

"This will be...my first time."

It was the deal breaker.

She knew it instantly. She could see it in his eyes—a sudden coolness.

"A virgin." He said it quietly. Flatly.

"What? Is there something wrong with being a virgin?" An inappropriate laugh tried to escape her. Somehow, she managed to hold it back.

"Elena." He said her name much too patiently. "No. There's nothing wrong with being a virgin. Nothing at all."

She sighed. "All of a sudden, you sound like somebody's father." The magic, most definitely, was gone.

He shifted beside her, putting a little distance between them. "Look. How about if I tell you what I was going to say? Then maybe you'll understand a little better why it bothers me that this would have been your first time."

Would have been. So there was no mistaking the situation. Lovemaking had been canceled due to her virginity. "Fire away."

"That first moment I saw you, standing next to the front desk at your dad's office...?"

"I remember."

"I knew I wanted you. I knew it was going to be really hard to keep my hands off you."

She couldn't help smiling then. "I felt the same—well, I mean, except that I had no plans to keep my hands off *you*."

"Listen." He looked so earnest, suddenly. So sincere. She remembered all the reasons she really, really liked him. "I want to make love with you. A lot. I like you, a lot. But I want a life on my own more than anything. I want some time to myself, you know? I've spent the last ten years being responsible to everyone—I've been running a business. *And* I've been a substitute dad. I want some time to be a single guy, with no one waiting at home for me. I need at least a couple of years where, beyond earning a living and building my business, I'm commitment-free."

"You think I want to take that away from you? If you do, you're wrong. I don't."

He started to reach out, thought better of it and lowered his hand without touching her. "Of course you don't. But you would. That's who you are, Elena. You're the woman a guy chooses for a lifetime. You're not someone who spends the night with a guy and then walks away in the morning."

She pressed her fingers to her temples, shook her head. "How can I be both flattered and insulted at the same time? That has to be impossible, right? But still. I am."

"I'm sorry," he said.

She groaned. "Why doesn't that help?"

"Listen. This isn't something you want to get into with me."

"Could you please not tell me what I want?"

"When I'm finished making this deal with your dad, it would be over with us. I would be gone and that would be it. You wouldn't be changing my mind. Are you willing to accept that?"

She stared at him. Oh, she was so tempted to insist that

she *was* willing—even if she wasn't. Tempted to take tonight and glory in it. And try her very best to get him to see things differently before he left San Antonio.

Slowly, she shook her head. "No." It was one thing if it didn't work out. She could accept that. But to go into it knowing his heart would be closed against her? Uh-uh. "I think you'd better just go."

"Yeah." He stood.

She got up, too, and followed him to the front door.

Before he left her, she caught his arm. "Wait."

"Elena..." The regret in his eyes was as clear as the yearning.

She went on tiptoe and kissed him. One last kiss, a deep, slow one, their tongues twining together, her breath coming faster...

But then, before it went beyond a kiss, she dropped back on her heels and stepped away. "Goodbye, Rogan."

With a last nod, he left her.

Mercy called the next morning as Elena was getting ready for school. The first words out of her mouth were, "Well? How was it?"

Elena told her sister the truth. "It was great. But we're not going out again."

"Huh? You have to know that makes no sense at all."

"Well, whether it makes sense or not, that's how it worked out."

"Want to talk about it?"

"Uh-uh." Elena had decided she was moving on. She was not going to dwell on what might have been.

"I'm here," Mercy offered. "Ready to listen if you change your mind."

"I know. And I appreciate that."

"I had such high hopes for him." Mercy sipped something—probably the hot water with lemon she'd been drink-ing in the mornings since she learned she was pregnant again. There was a crunching sound: saltines, no doubt.

Elena said, "Well, sometimes things just don't end up the way you wish they would—how are you feeling, anyway?"

Mercy put up no argument about the change of subject. "Mostly good. But, ugh, the morning sickness. It's worse than with Lucas."

Elena sympathized.

And when she hung up, she felt proud of herself. Yes, she was disappointed over the situation with Rogan. Very. To have finally felt that special something with someone. And then to have to accept that it wasn't happening, that you and the other person wanted different things.

But she hadn't cried on her sister's shoulder. She hadn't made a big deal of it. And she hadn't even mentioned her interest in Rogan to anyone else.

It really *wasn't* a big deal, just a date. One date. A lovely date. The best.

At least until the end.

She went to work, concentrated on her classes and her students. And got through the day well enough. True, the world seemed a little bit grayer, somehow. A little less vivid.

The sense of promise, of anticipation, that had buoyed her since she met Rogan last Friday afternoon was gone.

But it was okay. In a week, she'd be asking herself, "Rogan who?"

Life was not passing her by. She just hadn't met the right guy yet. And anyway, who needed a guy? She had a good life, a full one, just as it was.

After school, she had a Young Historians meeting and from there, she went to the gym. There was a certain guy, a cute pediatrician, who came in to use the weight machines around the same time she did.

They started talking, joking around. He asked her if she wanted to go out and get some dinner later.

She said she'd love to. They agreed to meet at a restaurant on the River Walk at seven-thirty. He was waiting when she got there.

It was…nice.

Nice, and nothing more. When they parted, he said he hoped they could have dinner again sometime. She nodded and smiled and left it at that.

At home, she congratulated herself on getting right back out there. She worked on her lesson plans, graded papers. Went to bed early.

Life was good, she reminded herself. Rich. Satisfying. She didn't need Rogan Murdoch to make it all complete.

Wednesday was a gray day, the sky heavy with clouds, promising rain.

During second period, one of the hall monitors came in with a note for her from the principal, Loretta Singh. Loretta needed to speak with Elena immediately.

Elena felt a little shiver of apprehension, like a trickle of ice water down her spine. Loretta never called a teacher to the office in the middle of class unless there was some major problem that had to be dealt with immediately.

An irate parent, a family emergency…

Whatever the issue was, it wouldn't be good.

She turned the class over to one of her star students and headed for the office, walking fast, her poor heart going a mile a minute, her stomach tied in one big, hard knot.

She knew when she stepped into Loretta's office that it was going to be really bad.

And it was.

Loretta spoke gently. "Elena." She smiled, but her eyes were shadowed. "Please. Sit down."

Sit down. It was what people always told you to do before they delivered the kind of information that could make your knees buckle.

Elena felt for the guest chair and eased herself down into it.

Once she was safely seated, Loretta spoke again. "I just got a call from a Mr. Murdoch."

Rogan? Had something happened to Rogan? Or maybe his sister or one of his brothers? But if it had, why would he be calling her? It made no sense.

No. It had to be someone in *her* family. *Papi*? Caleb or Irina? Dread squeezed her heart like a vise.

Loretta continued. "Mr. Murdoch asked me to tell you that your father's had a heart attack."

My father, she thought numbly. And then she wondered, *Papi? Davis?* As much as she wanted to deny her relationship to Davis, right at that moment, she had no idea which father Loretta meant.

Loretta added, "It happened at Cabrera Construction, he said. Your father's business?" *Papi.* Oh, God. It was *Papi* then. "Elena, would you like something…some water? Are you—?"

Elena waved a hand. "It's okay. I'm…I need to know. Where is my father now?"

"Elena—"

"Really. Please. Where is my father?"

"He's being rushed to Sisters of Mercy Hospital."

Chapter Six

At Sisters of Mercy, they sent her to the third floor, the cardiac unit.

The open waiting area was on a wide balcony that overlooked the floors below. There, families sat huddled together, trying to read magazines, looking drawn and worried, speaking in hushed tones.

Elena's mom had arrived before her. Luz was dressed for work in a slim skirt, high heels and a white silk shirt. Around her neck she wore the triple strand of Mikimoto pearls Javier had given her eight years ago to mark their twenty-fifth anniversary. Maybe Luz's presence should have surprised her, but it didn't. Elena knew that when disaster struck, the first person her dad would call would be Luz.

Rogan sat beside Luz. And another man, a little younger, sat beside him. Even with her mind eaten up with worry for her father, Elena knew who the other man was:

Cormac. Rogan's brother. He had the same green eyes and square jaw.

The men stood as Elena approached.

Luz jumped up, too, and held her arms wide. "Oh, *m'hija…*"

Elena ran to her and gathered her close. "*Mami…*" She wanted to cry. Crying would have been a relief. But somehow, the tears wouldn't come.

Luz took her by the shoulders. "Your sister and Luke are on the way." Her eyes were wet. She blinked, as if willing the tears away. But one escaped and trickled down her cheek.

Elena reached up and smudged it away with her thumb. "Dad…?"

Her mom's mouth trembled. "We don't know. He's still in surgery."

"But…he's going to be okay, right? He's going to be fine?"

Luz touched the side of Elena's face. "Yes. He will. I *know* he will." She spoke with conviction. But there was a world of worry in her eyes.

Elena grabbed her close again, hugged her so hard, whispered, "I'm so scared, *Mami.…*"

Luz rubbed her back, stroked her hair. "I know, I know. Shh, now. It's okay. We'll be strong. *Recias,* eh?"

Elena pulled back and drew herself up. Her mom was right. They had to show fortitude. Falling apart at this point wouldn't help her dad—or anyone else, for that matter. "Yes," she answered firmly. "Very strong." She turned to the two brothers, still standing side-by-side. "Hello, Rogan." They shared a nod. "And you must be Cormac."

Rogan's brother took her hand. "Elena. I wish we could have met under better circumstances."

"Me, too. I, um, take it you were both with him…when it happened?"

"At your dad's office, yes," Cormac confirmed.

"Come on," said her mother, putting a coaxing hand at her back. "Let's all sit down.…"

So they sat in a row—Luz, Elena, Rogan and Cormac. Luz felt for Elena's hand. They held on to each other, good and tight. It helped, a little.

Down the row of chairs, a woman said, "It's been hours."

"Soon," whispered the man beside her. "I'm sure we'll hear some news soon."

Elena turned to Rogan. "How did it…" Her throat clutched. She had to swallow, hard, before she could finish the simple sentence. "Happen?"

Rogan met her gaze directly. She saw concern in his eyes. And deep sympathy, too. But of course, he would understand. He'd lost both his parents, after all.

He knew what this horror felt like, knew much too well. "We were in your dad's office, going over the profit and loss statements."

"Was he upset about something?"

Rogan shook his head. "He was laughing."

She blinked. "Laughing?"

"Yeah. Cormac had made some joke. I don't even remember it now. Your dad laughed. And then, all at once, he grabbed his left arm and stood up, so hard and fast that his desk chair went flying back and hit the wall behind him. He said his arm hurt. And then he started to fall."

Cormac said, "Rogan got to him, caught him before he hit the floor."

Rogan picked up the story again. "I got him over to the corner couch, kind of half dragging him, and eased him down onto his back. Cormac was on the phone by then, calling 911. Your dad grabbed the front of my shirt. He was having trouble breathing and his color was really bad, but he somehow managed to tell me that he wanted me to call your mother—and you and your sister. After that, he faded out on us. I gave him CPR. But only briefly. The paramedics came fast."

"That's good!" She said it a little too loud, a little too desperately.

"Oh, yeah." He nodded, his gaze locked with hers. She knew he was willing her to believe—that her dad was going to make it. That for her, the horror would have a better ending than it had for him.

Her mother let go of her hand and stood again. "Mercedes..."

Elena looked over and Mercy and Luke were coming toward them. She got up, hugged Luke as her sister and mother embraced, then hugged her sister, too. It seemed a little ridiculous, all this hugging.

At the same time, it felt absolutely necessary.

They all sat down. Rogan introduced his brother to Mercy and Luke. And then they told the story of what had happened at the office again.

Luz asked after Lucas. Mercy said that Aleta was with him.

The waiting began anew, punctuated by ringing cell phones answered in hushed tones.

"Yes, he's still in surgery...."

"No, not yet."

"We'll call as soon as we know...."

Lunchtime came and went. They decided to take turns going down to the cafeteria in the basement—except for Luz. She refused to leave the waiting area. And then nobody really wanted to get up and leave. It seemed too dangerous to go. Something momentous might happen in their absence. The doctor could finally appear and tell them that Javier was going to be fine.

Or not.

Finally, Rogan and Cormac went downstairs together. They were back in ten minutes with sandwiches and fruit and bags of chips, enough for everyone. They passed the food around.

"Eat," Rogan commanded, when Luz tried to wave her sandwich away. "Just a few bites, at least. You need nourishment, Luz. To keep your strength up."

She gave in and took the food. He held out a sandwich to Elena next. Ham and cheese on wheat, she noticed. Not that it mattered. At that point, it was fuel. Period.

"Thank you," she whispered, and then, because it somehow didn't seem like enough, she said it again. "Thank you."

He nodded. She hoped he knew what she meant: *Thank you for everything. For being there when my dad needed you, for being here now.*

After everyone got food, Rogan took drink orders and hit the vending machines.

They ate—not a lot, but at least they made a pretense of it.

It was like a picnic, in a macabre sort of way. The kind of picnic Elena desperately hoped she'd never be involved in again.

And then she found herself thinking that moments like this had their own kind of value. With the threat of death so near, she felt frighteningly alive. And connected, deeply connected—to her mom and her sister, to Luke. And to Rogan, too. And even to Cormac, whom she had just met.

When the meal was done, they waited some more.

A woman doctor appeared—but not her dad's surgeon, Luz said. The doctor went and knelt in front of one of the other groups. A woman in that group gasped and burst into tears.

A man held her as she cried.

They all got up and followed the doctor away.

Elena ached for that family. She kept seeing her dad's face last Sunday, on Easter morning. How tired and old he'd looked. Should she have known that this was coming? It seemed now, in hindsight, that she should have. That all of the signs had been there. Since he and her mom had separated, he really hadn't been taking very good care of himself.

Finally, at 4:26 according to the clock on the wall, another doctor emerged. Luz rose at the sight of him and the rest of them followed her lead. That doctor came right for them. A tall, pale-haired man in green scrubs, with a mask hanging off one ear.

When he reached them, he spoke to her mother. "Mrs. Cabrera, your husband is…" The doctor continued speaking, but Elena's heart was beating so loudly, making a roaring in her ears, that his words came out in a weird, rushing blur.

She did get that her dad had made it through the surgery. A quintuple bypass. That soon they would be moving him to the Cardiac ICU. He was disoriented, the doctor said, but conscious. And he was asking for his wife.

Elena and Mercy had moved in close on either side of Luz. Each took an arm, to support their mother—and at the same time, it seemed to Elena, to hold each other up.

Luz whispered something under her breath. A fervent prayer of thanks, it sounded like. Then she asked the doctor, "My daughters? Would it be all right if they came in, too? They need to see their father, to know that he is all right."

"Of course," said the doctor. "Follow me."

They went, holding on to each other. The men, already

getting out their cell phones, stayed behind in the waiting room.

Down a long hallway and through a set of wide steel doors, they entered a small room full of equipment and nurses. It was the room where they took patients right after surgery. Four curtains on tracks hung from the ceiling. Two of those curtains were drawn aside, the areas within empty, except for all that equipment. But in the far corner, a curtain was pulled shut.

There was a gurney bed behind that curtain—Elena could see the steel legs. Someone was groaning in there. And there were hospital personnel around the patient. She could see their duty shoes, the cuffs of their scrub pants.

She wondered if she and her mom and her sister should be in here dressed in their street clothes. Was that safe?

But the doctor had brought them here. It must be okay.

The fourth curtain was half-drawn. She saw that just about every machine in there was hooked up to the man on the bed. And she saw graying hair on a pillow. Another step and she saw her dad's white, drawn face, his half-closed eyes. He looked so small to her in that rolling steel-railed bed, so small and wasted.

But then he saw her mother. His eyes opened all the way. And his too-pale face seemed to light up from within. He tried to speak around the breathing tube. All that came out was a croak. But there was no doubt that whatever he meant to say, it was something tender. Something loving. And his hand moved against the sheet that covered him, fingers reaching in spite of all the tubes hooked to the back of it.

And Elena knew then, she was absolutely certain. That he was going to be all right. That he and her mother would reunite. That sometimes the impossible can come true, in spite of the most terrible betrayals.

If there is love enough.

If there is real forgiveness.

Her mother said, in a voice of such love and pain—and such hope, "Javi..." And she went to his side.

Mercy and Elena hung back. They held on to each other as their mother laid her hand over their father's hand, as she bent close and pressed a gentle, awkward kiss on his top lip, above where the breathing tube protruded, as she whispered something only he could hear.

He was nodding. A tear dribbled down out of the corner of his eye. He tried to speak again. He said something in Spanish. Maybe "*Siempre.*" Always...

Or maybe something else.

Elena felt her own tears then, sliding down her cheeks. She looked at her sister. Mercy was crying, too. Simultaneously, they swiped at the tears with the backs of their hands.

Already, Javier was fading out, his eyes drooping shut. But he seemed to see them, his daughters, at the foot of the bed. Did he smile at them?

Elena thought he had tried to.

In the other bed, behind the curtain, the machines started beeping louder and faster. Someone in there cried out.

The doctor had disappeared. But a nurse touched Elena's arm, instructed softly, "Come with me, please. Mrs. Cabrera, you need to come, too. I'll take you back to the waiting area. As soon as Mr. Cabrera is comfortable in ICU, you'll be able to see him again."

Rogan watched as the three women, still holding on to each other, reappeared from the hallway past the elevators. Luz's face had a glow about it. Elena and Mercy were red-eyed, clutching tissues, dabbing at their cheeks. But he knew, mostly from the expression on Luz's face, that things were looking up.

Luke was already on his feet. His wife ran to him. He gathered her into his arms as a sob escaped her. She clung to him and he kissed her black hair. "Hey. Hey…" When she looked up at him, he cradled her face and pressed a cherishing kiss on her upturned mouth.

"He's going to make it, Luke, I just know it," Mercy whispered.

"Good," her husband said, and kissed her again. "Good."

Watching them, Rogan couldn't help thinking that closeness like that with the right woman would almost be worth the price of getting himself tied down again.

But not quite, he reminded himself. A man needed a little freedom. A man needed a few years in his life that belonged to him and him alone.

He glanced away—and right at Elena, who waited nearby, holding on to her mother's arm. Even with her eyes and nose all red and puffy from crying, she was way too damn beautiful for his peace of mind. He asked, "Good news, huh?"

She sniffed away the last of her tears. "He looks…like he just had open heart surgery. But yeah." She blew out a slow breath. "He came through all right."

"He's going to get well," her mother said. "I will see to it. And he'll be taking a lot better care of himself from now on." Rogan thought that even death wouldn't have a chance against the determination in Luz Cabrera's dark eyes.

And it was time for him and his brother to go. He glanced back at Cormac.

Cormac arched an eyebrow. "Ready?"

"Yeah. Just about." Rogan turned to Elena again. "Got a sec?"

Those thick, silky lashes swept down. And then she looked at him full-on again, wariness in her gaze. He thought she might refuse a moment alone with him. But then she forced a smile.

"Sure." She let go of her mom's arm.

He led her away from the waiting area, in the opposite direction of the elevators.

Around a corner, out of sight of the rest of them, there was a wide window overlooking the street below. He went to the window. It was raining, a drizzly sort of rain. The sky was thick with low-bellied dark clouds.

She faced him, one hand on the railing that ran beneath the window. "I know I said it earlier, but I don't see how it can hurt to say it again. I'm so glad that you and Cormac were there when it happened. You saved my dad's life. I can't tell you how grateful I am."

He put up a hand. "Seriously. It's not a big thing. Anyone would have—"

"Uh-uh." She was looking down now, at the tightly woven industrial gray carpet beneath their feet, shaking her head, her shining hair falling forward. "I don't know what *anyone* would have done." Guiding the thick curls back behind her ears, she looked at him again. "I know what *you* did. You saved my dad's life. Thank you."

He wanted to reach for her, to pull her close, to tip up her chin and kiss her—a long, slow, deep kiss. But of course, he didn't. They knew where they stood with each other and they weren't going there. "Well, all right. You're welcome."

"And if there's ever anything I can do for you, just say the word. I'll be there." Her whiskey-brown eyes held no double meanings.

Which was good, he told himself. They understood each other. There would be no kissing. Not now. Not ever.

"Okay," he said. "I'll remember that." He stuck his hands in his back pockets and chuckled low.

"What's funny?"

"It's just that you beat me to the punch. I dragged you over here to tell you that if you needed anything—anything at all—you just have to call me."

She smiled then, a warm, open smile. He spotted that dimple he'd always admired. "Well. Okay, Rogan. I'll do that."

He slid a card from his breast pocket and gave it to her. She took it by the corner. Their fingers didn't touch. "My cell's on there. And the office number, which is in Fort Worth. And for now, I'm at the Palicio del Rio Hilton."

"I remember. You told me."

He added, "We'll be there for a while, depending on how your dad is doing and how long it takes us to wrap up the deal."

"So, the sale is a go?"

"I think it's safe now to say that it is."

"Good. I know it's what my dad wants...." Her voice trailed off.

Outside, a bolt of lightning pierced the clouds. Thunder rumbled. Rain drizzled down the wide window pane. The scent of her came to him, faintly, a sweet, tempting echo of what might have been.

There was nothing more to say. "Take care of yourself, okay?"

Her smile was brave and bright. "You, too."

They went back to the others. Rogan and Cormac said goodbye and headed for the elevators.

Elena watched him go and longed to chase after him, to tell him that she did need something, as a matter of fact. She needed him. Now. Here, by her side.

Once they'd disappeared from view, Mercy gestured over her shoulder, in the direction Elena and Rogan had gone to speak privately. "What was *that* about?"

Elena only smiled. "He just wanted to wish me well."

"He's a good man," their mother said and Mercy made a low noise of agreement.

"Yeah. He is." Elena stared off toward the elevators, way too aware of his absence now that he was gone.

Sisters of Mercy had a patient-centered Cardiac ICU, so Luz could spend a lot of time with her husband, could be there, be involved, any time a decision had to be made concerning his care.

And at night, the hospital provided a sleeping area, where spouses could stay over, to be nearby in case of any after-hours emergencies. Luz remained at the hospital round-the-clock. Mercy, Luke and Elena were in and out.

Elena took family leave for the rest of the week. And since the next week, the first week in May, would be spring vacation and Cinco de Mayo, she'd be free then, too. She could be with the family, stick close to her dad.

Javier improved relatively quickly. He was out of ICU in twenty-four hours. In his new room, Luz could stay with him all the time.

Maybe it was happiness that speeded his recovery. He and her mom were like a couple of newlyweds, holding hands, whispering together. Suddenly, her mom looked ten years younger.

Friday, Marcella came to see him. And a couple of sub-contractors who worked with him.

And later in the afternoon, Elena's half sister, Abilene Bravo McCrae stopped in to see how he was doing.

Abilene was an architect. The year before, she'd worked with Elena's dad at Cabrera Construction, drafting house plans for him, sometimes even supervising at building sites. She and Javier were good friends—and yet another example of the many connections between the Bravo and Cabrera families.

She brought her new husband with her, the famous architect, Donovan McRae.

Donovan had been in an accident a couple of years before and sustained serious damage to his legs. He could walk now, using a cane. But most of the time, he got around in a wheelchair. He said that the chair was a lot easier than limping around on his messed up legs. He wheeled into Javier's hospital room behind his wife. Abilene took one side of the bed and Donovan the other.

The couple stayed for an hour, joking with Javier, reporting on the progress of the children's center they were building. Elena and her mom were there at the time. They stood back out of the way, letting the visitors enjoy their time with him.

Elena watched Abilene and her husband together. They were clearly a great match, with so much in common. And totally in love. Whenever they glanced at each other, you could feel the connection between them, the excitement— and the affection, too.

Lately, it seemed like everywhere she looked she saw a couple in love. Her mom and her dad. Mercy and Luke. Abilene and Donovan.

She was happy for them. She truly was.

But she did wonder if her turn for true love would ever come.

And that got her thinking about Rogan, about how he was the right man at the wrong time—the wrong time for him, anyway.

How much freedom would be enough for him? How long

until he'd had his fill of being footloose and unencumbered by love or commitment?

She could almost feel angry at him, for not wanting what she wanted. Even though she knew that wasn't the least bit fair.

But then, life wasn't fair.

Life was tough—and way too short.

She was achingly aware of how quickly life could be snuffed out. Her dearest *Papi* had almost died. He probably would have died, if not for the quick action on the part of the Murdoch brothers. Her dad could have died without ever getting to look in her mother's eyes again, without ever getting another chance to really *be* with her mother the way they were together now.

Because life was not only tough and short, it was unpredictable. A person needed to grab what she wanted when she had the chance. In the end, you just never knew if your chance would come around again.

At home that evening, she had a bunch of messages on her machine—people asking how her dad was doing, a couple of teachers from her school checking to see that she was hanging in there.

There was one from Caleb. She returned his call first.

"Hey, big brother."

"Hey. How's it going?"

"Really well. My dad may be going home Monday."

"Isn't that fast?"

"I think they say three to five days after getting out of ICU is average, so it's quick. But not out of the ordinary."

"That's terrific."

"Yeah."

He said, "Irina's doing her famous crown roast of lamb for dinner. Come on over. Join us."

Just what she needed. An evening with another perfectly matched loving couple. "Can I get a rain check?"

"You sure?"

"Yeah. Think I'll put my feet up, watch a little Lifetime channel."

"You don't know what you're missing—but I get it. You probably need a little downtime about now."

"That is exactly what I need." And a little time away from blissfully happy couples.

He told her to call. Anytime. For anything. She promised she would and they said goodbye.

She returned the other calls—all but one. From Davis.

It wasn't the first time he'd called her. Or the second. In the past couple of years, he'd been calling her home phone every couple of months or so, on average. Often enough that she'd gotten into the habit of screening her calls to keep from having to deal with him, and of hitting the delete button automatically when he left a message, without even listening to what he had to say.

This time, though, she sat at the breakfast bar that separated her kitchen from the dining area and she played his message back.

"Hello, Elena." His voice, as always, so deep and commanding—and maybe a little bit nervous, too. "I only wanted to let you know that I've been thinking about you. I heard that Javier is going to pull through and I'm really happy to hear that. Happy to know that…well, that everything is all right, or will be, in time. And I…guess that's all. Please take care of yourself and call me if you need anything, if there's anything I can do." He rattled off a couple of phone numbers. And then he said, "Goodbye."

Click. Dial tone.

Elena punched the reset button. And then she just sat there, staring at the machine. She'd heard nothing but sincerity in Davis's voice. Sincerity and the desire to help if she needed help. Sincerity and the need to know his own daughter.

Really. Life was too damn short.

She picked up the phone and she dialed the first number he had given in his message.

He answered on the second ring. "This is Davis."

"Hi. Um, it's Elena."

A huge, echoing silence. And then a sharply indrawn breath. "Elena. Hello." He sounded shocked. And so very pleased.

She smiled to herself and held the phone a little tighter. "I got your message. Thank you."

"Ahem. Well, yes. I wanted to check on you, to make sure you're doing all right."

"I am."

"Javier?" A note of worry crept into his voice. "Has something happened?"

"He's doing great. Really well."

"Well. Good. Excellent. I'm glad to hear it."

"And actually, Davis, I called because I was..." How to say it? How to begin?

"Yes?" He sounded so hopeful it almost hurt to hear him.

She went ahead with it. "I was also thinking about...I don't know. Lunch, maybe?"

Another silence. And then a swift, "Yes. Yes, I would like that."

"Tomorrow?"

"Tomorrow. Well, that's great. Perfect. What time?"

"Noon?"

"Noon is good."

She named a restaurant. "Do you know it?" She named the street.

"I can find it. I'll be there."

"Great. I'll call and make sure we have a table."

"Okay. Yes. Good."

"And I'll…see you then."

"Yes. Well, then. Goodbye, Elena."

"Goodbye, Davis."

He hung up. And slowly, quietly, she set the phone down.

She felt the strangest happy glow within. The kind you feel when you know that you've taken a big step in the right direction.

Truly. Life was too short.

She glanced at her watch. Nearly seven. She supposed she ought to start thinking about putting something together for dinner. She had her mother's famous recipe for pork chile verde, already made, in the freezer. A lot of it. Burritos, maybe. And a salad.

Way, way too short…

She put her head down on her arms, shut her eyes, let out a little moan of indecision.

Too short…

And when she sat up straight again, the first thing her gaze fell on was the small corkboard on the wall above the phone and the business card she'd pinned up there when she got home late Wednesday night.

Rogan's card.

She took the card off the corkboard and carried it with her into her bedroom, where she pulled open the drawer in the nightstand.

The box of condoms was way in the back. She'd bought them when she was going out with Tonio, before she started on the pill.

Just in case…

Now, of course, she'd been on the pill for weeks, much

longer than the initial seven days during which her doctor had warned her she also needed to use some other form of contraception.

However, she'd kind of gotten off her schedule, had missed a pill yesterday, after her dad had his heart attack.

So what, she'd thought this morning when she'd discovered she'd skipped a dose.

It didn't matter.

Or it hadn't.

Until tonight, when she'd started obsessing over all she was missing.

But then again, she had the condoms. She should be perfectly safe.

And besides, even with a missed pill, the risk was miniscule.

As slowly as she had put down the kitchen extension, she picked up the one in the bedroom.

Chapter Seven

Twenty minutes after she called him, Rogan stood at Elena's door, ringing the bell.

The door swung open so fast, he wondered if she'd been standing on the other side of it waiting for him. "Rogan. Hi. Um, thanks so much for coming."

Words seemed to have deserted him. He managed to speak her name. "Elena."

And then, for several endless seconds, they just stood there at her threshold, staring at each other.

How was it that every time he saw her she seemed to get more beautiful? She wore curve-hugging jeans and a sleeveless silk shirt with a deep neckline. It was white, that shirt, printed with little red hearts, a spill of ruffles down the front. Her hair was loose and thick on her shoulders.

It couldn't be fair for a woman to look that good.

Finally, she stepped back and ushered him in. He followed behind her, through the open living area, past the dining table set for two, to the kitchen.

Something smelled really good.

His stomach growled. Was there going to be dinner? He'd been just about to order up room service when she called.

"Would you like a beer?" she asked. He nodded. She got a tall one from the fridge, opened it, passed it to him. "Have a seat." She indicated the counter that divided off the kitchen.

He sat. Sipped. "So…what's happened?"

She stirred a pot on the stove—the source, he realized, of that wonderful smell. "Hungry?"

"Starving. But you said there was a favor you needed from me…."

The lid clattered a little as she set it back on the pot. Carefully, she set her wooden spoon in the spoon rest. She looked…kind of pale. Kind of stricken.

He got up from his stool. "Elena. What is it?"

She patted the air with both hands. "I'm sorry. I didn't mean to scare you."

"But you *are* scaring me. If there's something I can do, you need to tell me. You need to——"

"Rogan."

"What?"

"It's…difficult."

"What?"

She raked that fabulous hair back with her fingers. "Could you just…finish your beer? Could we just eat first?"

He sank back on the stool. Okay. So she needed a little time to tell him about it—whatever the hell *it* was. Fine. He picked up his beer, knocked back a big slug of it, set it down. "Sure."

So they ate. The food was really good.

After the meal, they went over and sat on the couch together.

"Another beer?" she offered.

He shook his head. "Is this about your dad? Has something gone wrong?"

"No. He's doing well. Really well. Better every day." She slipped off her flat red shoes and drew up her slender, pretty feet. Her toenails were as red as her shoes. Bright red. Sexy red. "This is…" She drew in a big breath and blew her cheeks out as she released it. "I have no idea where to begin. I really, truly don't."

Now he wanted to comfort her, for some odd reason. But then, he had that feeling a lot when it came to her. He also wanted to tear off her clothes and carry her to the nearest bed.

She was dangerous to him, big-time. Dangerous to his plans of independence and reduced responsibility. He knew that.

He should find out what she needed, get it for her, and get the hell away from her. "Just go for it." *Please.*

"Life is short," she said, as if that explained anything.

"That's right. It is. And?"

"And everybody I know is half of a loving, happy couple. They're all crazy about each other, so glad to be together. My sister has a darling little boy and a baby on the way. My half sister, Zoe, is pregnant and due to deliver any second now." He remembered Zoe, the pretty, very pregnant redhead. He'd met her and her husband Easter Sunday. Elena was still talking. "Zoe's madly in love with her husband, Dax. And my other half sister, Abilene? Married. Totally in love. Six of my seven half brothers? Them, too. And Davis and Aleta. Even my parents—they're back together, 'id you hear? More solid than they ever were."

"I'm not surprised," he said cautiously. "It was pretty

clear, even to an outsider, that they still love each other."
Where was this going? He had the strangest feeling it was
somewhere he shouldn't allow it to go.

But how to stop her? She seemed to be on a roll. "Too
short," she said again, "too, too short." She was shaking
her head, all that glorious hair that he only wanted to bury
his face in, catching the lamplight, strands of gold and red
glinting in the sable brown. "And Rogan, I've been a virgin
for too long, you know? I want…what other women have.
Heat. Passion. The thrill, you know?"

He gaped. He was suddenly pretty sure where she was
leading him. Somewhere he knew there was no way he
could go. "Elena, I think you should—"

She went right on as if he hadn't tried to say something.
"At least that, the passion. If I can't have it all, I at least want
to know what it's like with a man. With the *right* man." She
pinned him with those big brown eyes. "With you."

"Uh…"

She licked her lips.

Heat flashed to his groin. Okay. He knew he should get
out of there. Yes, he did. But somehow, he didn't move. He
couldn't take his eyes off her. She amazed him. She had it
all. Goodness. Truthfulness. Beauty. Brains.

He was thinking the last thing he should let himself
think: *Okay. She's worth it. Whatever the price.*

"Rogan." She canted toward him. He caught the scent
of her. So good. So tempting. "I want you," she said. "I
want…us. Just for a little while. Just for as long as you're
here in San Antonio. I know that you're leaving as soon as
you buy out my dad. I accept that. I can live with that. I can
let you go with…a full heart. Without putting any pressure
on you to be someone you don't want to be right now. I
can—I *will* let you go and not try to hold you. Let you g
and just be glad for what we had. I…" The flood of wor

had finally run dry. She let out a low, tight little moan and sank back to her side of the couch. "I…" She put a hand against her flushed cheek. "Oh, God. Will you please just *say* something? Say anything, *now*."

"Elena, I…" He felt breathless, suddenly, as if he'd run up a high, steep hill.

"Yes. What? Tell me." She leaned into him again, bringing the scent of gardenias and honeysuckle. Her eyes were amber, hot as flame.

"Are you sure about this?"

"Yes. I am. Totally certain. I understand that it's just for now. Until you go. I…accept your terms."

"It's only…"

"What? Only what?"

"I don't want to take advantage of you."

"Advantage?" She made a sharp sound. Like a laugh and a cry at once. "How can you be taking advantage of me if you give me what I want, what I ask for, what I really, really need right now?"

"Elena, I don't think that we—"

She silenced him with her soft hand across his mouth. "Look. If you want to say no, just say it. I can accept a no. But don't you try to be nice about it. Don't try to let me down easy." She spoke through clenched teeth. "Just do it. Just say it and let it be." Her hot gaze pinning him, she lowered her hand.

A voice in his head commanded: *Get up. Leave. Do it now.*

He did no such thing.

What he did was reach for her.

He slid his hand under the warm, silky fall of her hair clasped the back of her neck.

ith a moan, she swayed toward him.

And in that instant, he was lost. He surrendered. Completely.

He pulled her against him and fastened his mouth on hers.

She opened, sighing. He tasted her, spearing his tongue in. She met him, sliding her tongue along his, welcoming him.

How pointless, he thought, to have tried to refuse her. They had been leading to this moment from the beginning. From that afternoon in her father's office. From the first time he looked into her eyes.

It had been bound to happen. No escaping.

No turning away.

He framed her warm, sweet face in his palms. "Elena…"

"Oh, Rogan. Oh, yes…"

He kissed her again, a quick kiss. He didn't dare linger right then. If he did, he wouldn't stop until he had every stitch of clothing off her, until he had her naked beneath him and he was buried, all the way, in her softness. Until he lost himself in her.

But no. Not this time. Not for her *first* time.

He took her shoulders, stiffened his arms enough to push her away from him.

She blinked like a woman in a dream. "What? Is something wrong?"

"Nothing's wrong," he said. "Everything's right." A few strands of gold-shot sable hair were caught on her eyelashes. With a careful touch of a finger, he freed them. "Let's go to bed."

Her smile bloomed slowly, that dimple appearing, sh\ as a sliver of moon on a cloudy night. "Okay."

He trailed a hand down the silky flesh of her arr capture her hand. "Come on." He got up.

She eased her bare feet to the floor and rose with him. He led the way, around the coffee table, through the arch to the little square of hallway and the door to her bedroom.

The bed was already turned back, the lights seductively low. He smiled to himself, picturing her rushing around, getting everything ready.

For him.

For the two of them, together.

They stood facing each other, in about the same place they had stood a few nights ago, on the thick rug by the turned-back bed. But a few nights ago, they had reconsidered the wisdom of carrying things too far. And he had left her.

He would not be leaving tonight.

Dragging her close again, he wrapped his arms around her and claimed a kiss. But it didn't last long enough. She pressed her hands against his chest. "Let me…"

"Whatever you want." He moved back a step.

She unbuttoned his shirt, tugging the shirttail free of his trousers, sliding those soft hands upward again over his bare chest until her fingers curled around his shoulders and she eased the shirt down his arms.

The cuffs were still buttoned. The shirt got stuck at his wrists. But that didn't seem to bother her. She held his arms behind his back, a tender sort of bondage.

And she moved in close again, pressing those sweet lips to the center of his chest. She turned her head to the side, rubbed her hair against him, and then tipped her head up and gave him a beautiful, rueful smile. "I feel…so strange. I want this, with you. I want it so much. But I don't really have a clue what I'm doing."

"Coulda fooled me." His voice came out rough and low. 's head was filled with the smell of flowers. All she'd done was kiss his chest and rub that beautiful hair against his skin—and he was hard.

And getting harder. Aching. Needing…

She was still watching him, her face tipped up, her eyes heavy-lidded. "I think you're going to have to take it from here."

"Fair enough." He bent his head and caught her mouth again. She sighed and gave herself up to the kiss.

He took a long time about that kiss, enjoying the feel of her mouth under his, the arousing brush of ruffled silk against his bare chest, the ripe feel of her breasts under the smooth fabric. She might be new to this, but she sure had a talent for it.

She lifted those curvy hips to him, rubbing herself against him, making him harden for her all the more.

He wanted to grab her, take her down the bed.

But more than that, he wanted to go slow, to make her first time good for her.

Her first time.

His conscience jabbed at him. Her first time should be with a man who would swear never to leave her, a man who whispered words of love to her….

Though he was still kissing her, she must have sensed his mind's withdrawal.

She broke the kiss and gazed up at him again. "Don't stop. Please." She seemed to mean it.

This *was* what she wanted, he reminded himself. She'd made it more than clear. And as it happened, it was what he wanted, too—more than wanted. It was what he craved. "I won't," he whispered, bending close, nuzzling her temple, making himself drunk on the scent of her hair.

It didn't take a lot of effort to free his wrists from he grasp. He gave a tug; she let go. Stepping back, her fa solemn and dreamy at once, she allowed him to undo his cuffs and get rid of the shirt.

Her gaze ran over his bare chest, burning where it touched. Shyly, she suggested. "The pants, too?"

He was only too happy to oblige her. He undid his belt and his fly.

Her eyes got wider. She licked those full lips of hers, waiting.

He dropped trou—and then realized he probably should have taken off his boots first. Looking down over his boxers, he saw his bare, hairy legs and his pants in a pool around his ankles.

She gave a low laugh. "I think you need some help."

He glanced up into her waiting eyes. "You may be right."

She pushed him down on the bed. "I can handle this part." Her hair fell forward as she bent close.

He caught a shining lock of the stuff, rubbed it between his fingers. So warm, so alive. "A fast learner, huh?"

"I don't know about that. But I think I can manage to help you get your boots off."

He canted back on his elbows and stuck out a boot. "Great."

She went right to work. And she did a fine job of it, too, turning, hitching a leg over his, grabbing the heel and levering it up and off, pulling off his sock right after it, then repeating the process with the other boot. Not only was she quick and efficient, she looked really amazing from behind as she bent to her work. She pulled his already-lowered trousers off last.

When she turned back to him, he wore only his boxers, which didn't hide much—not at the moment. He was still lying back on his elbows. But a part of him was standing stiff. She had his complete attention.

She looked at the tented front of his boxers and caught her lower lip between her teeth. With apprehension?

He wasn't sure.

But he did know it was time for him to take the lead again. He swept to his feet. "Elena…" He took her by the shoulders.

She gazed up at him, wide-eyed, mouth curving in a trembling smile. "Uh. Hmm?"

"Any time you want to stop…"

"I don't."

"Good." He kissed the tip of her nose.

"There is something, though, something I need to say.…"

"Say it. Anything. It's okay."

"I have condoms, in that drawer there." She pointed to the nightstand at the head of the bed.

"You said you're on the pill."

"I am. But, well, I…" She was blushing furiously.

"You're right," he said. Better for both of them to be absolutely safe in every way. "Good thinking." He turned, pulled the drawer wide, took out the box, removed two pouches and set them next to the lamp. Then he put the box away. "There. All set."

She wrapped her arms around herself, rubbed her upper arms, as though the room had suddenly turned cold. "I feel…out of my depth, you know? Just totally in over my head."

Should he ask her again if she wanted to back out?

No. Enough. Unless she spoke up, they were going forward. "Shh." He took her by the shoulders. "Turn around."

"Um, why?"

He let go of her and arched a brow, but kept his mout

shut, giving her another chance to tell him if she'd finally admitted to herself that she just wasn't up for this.

"I...oh, of course, I don't need to know why. I'm...um." She coughed into her hand, a nervous and rather endearing little sound. "Never mind. Turning around. Doing it now." And then she whirled and faced away from him. "There." She dropped her hands to her sides, drew herself up straight and let out a shuddering little sigh. "Done."

He smiled to himself. "Excellent." He stepped in good and close. "Perfect."

Another trembling sigh escaped her. But she didn't say anything, only stood there, staring off toward the far wall, head held high.

He pulled her into him, wrapped his arms around her.

She felt so right there in his embrace. And she sighed again—an easier sound than before, and let herself settle back against him. He smoothed her hair out of the way and pressed his lips against the side of her neck. She moaned a little, tipping her head for him, offering him more.

He stuck out his tongue and tasted her skin. A little salty, temptingly sweet.

She glanced back at him then, turning her head enough that he could take her lips. And he did. He plundered them.

And his hands went exploring. He molded the fine, slim curve of her waist, trailing the caress upward until he could cup her breasts in his palms. They felt wonderful, soft and full—and warm, even through the protective layers of her shirt and bra.

She sighed some more, and then broke the kiss to let her head fall back against his shoulder. "Oh, Rogan..."

He murmured a low, wordless sound in response and let his hands slide downward again. Catching the hem of her pretty shirt, he eased it upward. Lazily, she raised her arms for him.

He took the wisp of shirt up and away. And then he clasped her upraised wrists. Her bones were so fine and small, her skin so warm, so impossibly smooth. He caressed his way down, over her forearms, her elbows, to the secret hollows beneath her arms.

And then inward, to her breasts again, now only hidden from him behind twin bits of black lace. He held them, cupping them once more, and used his thumbs to rub the swells of plump flesh above the lace.

She liked that. She murmured his name again and arched her back, pressing her breasts more fully into his cradling hands and also rubbing against him down low, driving him crazy, making him ache for her. With his thumbs, he eased the lace aside, revealing the hard, brown nipples he wanted to taste.

But no. It was better for her now, if she stayed with her back to him. He could caress her at will. And she could feel free to do nothing but respond.

He caught those pretty nipples between his thumbs and forefingers, pinched them a little, rolled them, teased them.

Her response was another deep, pleasured moan. She turned her head to him again. He took her offered mouth and kissed her some more.

He loved touching her, couldn't seem to get enough of the feel of her under his hands. He skimmed his fingers over her belly and lower, sliding them into the cove between her thighs. Even with her jeans still covering her, he could feel the heat.

She moved her hips into his touch and groaned into his mouth.

He took that as a sign to slip the snap free at the top of

her jeans, to slide the zipper down and pull it wide. She didn't object, so he figured it was safe to go further.

She wore tiny lacy panties. The flesh above them was firm and flat, velvet-smooth. He eased a finger under the elastic. She sucked in a quick breath, pulling her mouth from his so that she could lean more fully against him.

He pressed his lips into her hair, waited for a sign from her that she wanted more.

She gave it in a trembling whisper. "Please…"

He delved in. She felt like heaven. The scent of her was dizzying, muskier now. Sweeter even than before. He rubbed the thick curls that protected her sex, felt the silky wetness that told him everything he needed to know.

So he went lower.

Elena gasped as he parted the curls that covered her mound. She felt…revealed by him, somehow. Revealed *to* him, though he was behind her and couldn't see what his fingers were doing to her, though she still wore her panties and her jeans, as well.

Still, she felt *known* in an intimate, purely sexual way, for the first time.

And it felt so good, so exciting. So exactly as she had fantasized it might.

Oh, yes. Exactly.

Only better. Even better.

His clever, slightly rough, wonderful fingers moved lower still, between the secret folds of her most private flesh—not entering her. Not yet. Just…touching her, discovering her, stroking her, where she was wet and hot and slick, yearning for him.

Her whole body had gone electric and shimmery. A floating, glittery feeling. Like rays of sunlight flickering on the surface of a glassy pond. Her breasts ached in a wonderful, hungry way—the same as she ached in the slick, yearning place where he was touching her. An ache of pure pleasure, building. Gathering....

So right, so good, the way he touched her. And she loved the feel of him, of his big, strong body behind her, supporting her.

And teasing her, too, with the way he rubbed himself against her, with the simple proof of his wanting her—she could feel that also, feel the hard ridge of him through his boxers, through her jeans. It was pressing into her, making her ache even more deliciously, making her mindful of what was to come.

And down where he touched her...

Oh, that was something. She moaned deep in her throat as he went further, as he eased one clever finger inside. Her body tightened at that first small invasion.

But then she sighed. And she realized how good it felt, how perfectly right and natural. Her body opened enough to ease the way.

One finger...

And then another.

And then he was moving his hand, stroking her, doing impossible, lovely, stimulating things.

She arched against him, sliding her hands behind her, under his arms and around him, so she could grasp his hard, muscular hips and pull him closer, tighter to her. So she could feel him more acutely, there at the small of her back, at the same time as his fingers worked their magic on her, stroking her, arousing her so completely.

She was lost, oh yes.

Lost in the most perfect, delicious way. Every cell in her body was vibrating, as she moved her hips against his stroking hand and she felt that shimmer of pleasure gathering

GET 2 BOOKS

We'd like to send you two *Silhouette Special Edition*® novels absolutely free. Accepting them puts you under no obligation to purchase any more books.

HOW TO GET YOUR
2 FREE BOOKS AND 2 FREE GIFTS

1. Return the reply card today, and we'll send you two *Silhouette Special Edition* novels, absolutely free! We'll even pay the postage!

2. Accepting free books places you under no obligation to buy anything, ever. Whatever you decide, the free books and gifts are yours to keep, free!

3. We hope that after receiving your free books you'll want to remain a subscriber, but the choice is yours—to continue or cancel, any time at all!

EXTRA BONUS

You'll also get two free mystery gifts! (worth about $10)

FREE!

Return this card today to get
2 FREE BOOKS and 2 FREE GIFTS!

SPECIAL EDITION®

YES! Please send me 2 FREE *Silhouette Special Edition*®
novels, and 2 free mystery gifts as well. I understand
I am under no obligation to purchase anything, as
explained on the back of this insert.

*About how many NEW paperback fiction books have
you purchased in the past 3 months?*

❏ 0-2
E9TD

❏ 3-6
E9TP

❏ 7 or more
E9TZ

235/335 SDL

FIRST NAME	LAST NAME

ADDRESS

APT.#	CITY

Visit us at:
www.ReaderService.com

STATE/PROV.	ZIP/POSTAL CODE

◄ DETACH AND MAIL CARD TODAY!

(S-SE-03/11)

BUSINESS REPLY MAIL
FIRST-CLASS MAIL   PERMIT NO. 717   BUFFALO, NY

POSTAGE WILL BE PAID BY ADDRESSEE

THE READER SERVICE
PO BOX 1867
BUFFALO NY 14240-9952

NO POSTAGE
NECESSARY
IF MAILED
IN THE
UNITED STATES

into itself, tighter, more focused, building to something so perfect.

And then he touched the little bud of flesh at the top of her sex. He rubbed it with his thumb.

And that did it. That carried her up and over the crest. She shut her eyes, held his hips even tighter, closer against her. She tossed her head wildly on his shoulder, cried out his name.

He stayed with her, stroking her with those knowing fingers of his, as the pleasure burst wide open and she shuddered and moaned.

And then, as the wonder faded down to a golden glow, he skimmed off her jeans and her little panties, too. She stood there, dazed, in the lovely aftermath of pleasure, as he removed all the rest of her clothes.

When she was naked, he took her shoulders, turned her around to him and pulled her close.

His body to her body with nothing between them. She hadn't noticed when he took off his boxers. But he had. They were gone.

There was only his flesh, so firm and hot, only the strength in his arms, the thick muscles of his chest.

It was a revelation. So exactly what she'd hungered for.

She gazed up into his eyes, eyes as green as shamrocks, as new-cut grass. "Oh, Rogan…"

He kissed his name off her eager lips.

And then he guided her backwards until her knees met the edge of the mattress.

"Lie down, Elena." It was a tender command, but a command nonetheless.

She obeyed him. She was his in that moment, utterly. Completely. There was nothing he could have asked of her that she would not willingly have done. She scooted up on the bed and stretched out on the pillows as he took one of the condoms from the nightstand, unwrapped it and rolled it down over himself.

And then he came to her. He kissed her, so deeply. So thoroughly.

He kissed her throat and her breasts, her belly. And lower.

He kissed her everywhere.

And when he finally eased her thighs apart and settled between them, she was ready, open. Eager for him.

He was gentle with her.

But still, she felt pressure that became pain as he eased himself into her, so slowly. With such care. The barrier against him stretched, burning.

And then broke. She let out a sharp cry.

"Elena…" He wove his hands with hers, pinned them back against the pillows.

And he kissed her, his tongue stroking her, as below, he was so still.

So still, waiting.

For her body to give way to him, to accept him.

To go easy and ready around him.

It didn't take too long. The pain slid away, leaving a slight sting. And then the sting faded, too.

And there began to seem something right about the feel of him, filling her. Something good.

Something exciting.

She lifted her hips to him, just to see what it felt like to move—good.

It felt good.

She did it again.

He stiffened above her, moaned.

She smiled against his mouth, eased her hands from where he pinned them and wrapped her arms around his rib cage.

He braced his forearms beside her head, caught her face between his palms, lifted his mouth from hers. "Elena?" He looked stunned. Transfixed. "Are you…?"

"I am fine. Really. Better than fine." She wrapped her legs around him, too. With a groan, she pushed up to him, took him in all the way.

"Elena…" He said her name on a growl that time. "I can't…"

"Hold back? Then don't."

And that was it. The permission he needed. With a low moan, he buried his head against her neck and surged within her.

It hurt, a little, yes.

But she didn't care. There was wonder in it. Such tender, aching beauty.

She held on tight. She pushed her hips up, opening her thighs all the wider, welcoming him.

He pressed his mouth to the side of her throat, grazed her skin with his teeth, licked her, sucked hard enough that she thought he might leave a mark.

She didn't care. He was lost in her and she in him. She brought her hands inward, between them, and then caught his face, spearing her fingers into his close-cut hair, tugging him up to her, until he gave her his mouth again.

A long kiss and a wild ride.

He moved in her, so deeply. And when he withdrew it was only to come back to her, into her, so fully.

He moved faster. Deeper. He pressed his face against her throat again. She tried to keep up with him, to go with him, into the sweet magic of another finish.

But her untried body wasn't ready for that, not ready to let go again. It was all too new, too overwhelming. For then, all she could do was hold on, so tight.

And she found that it was enough, right then. To feel him

within her, to know that he wanted her so much, he forgot himself, forgot his careful and expert seduction.

That he gave himself up to her, surrendered himself. To her.

Until he let out a low, guttural sound against her neck, until he pushed in so hard and she strained upward, toward him, giving him all of herself.

Every hard muscle tight, he stilled deep inside her. And she felt him, felt the pulsing within her as he came.

She made a low sound in her throat, turned and pressed her lips against his sweat-slick temple and then wrapped her arms even tighter around him than before.

"Should have waited..." He groaned against her throat, panting a little as he caught his breath. "...for you."

"Don't worry." She laughed then, a low, husky sound. "There's always the next time...."

He rolled a little, pulling her with him, so he wasn't putting all his weight on her. And they lay there, facing each other on their sides in the soft glow of the bedside lamp, her leg wrapped across his thigh.

She still held him inside.

That seemed terribly intimate and lovely to her. The two of them, lying there, staring into each other's eyes, both of them panting, catching their breath.

Still connected.

He frowned and gently smoothed her hair behind her ear. "I should have taken it easier, been more gentle. I guess I kind of lost it there at the end."

She brushed a kiss across his lips. "Isn't that what you're supposed to do—lose it?"

"Only if *you're* losing it, too."

She put her hand up between them, touched his lips with the tips of her fingers. They were so soft, so unlike the rest of him, which was wonderfully muscled and manly. She whispered, "Such a thoughtful guy."

"I try."

She thought about how she *had* lost it, before they even got in bed. And then she marveled that she'd finally made love. With a good man. The *right* man.

She felt just great about her choice.

He touched her cheek with the sides of his fingers, the caress featherlight. "You seem thoughtful."

"It's been a scary, awful week in a lot of ways. But everything looks a lot brighter now. I feel…happy right now, Rogan. Just plain happy."

"That's good."

"That's excellent." *Lover,* she thought. He is my lover. A little thrill shivered down her spine.

He shifted a little and she felt him slip away from her. There was suddenly wetness on the inside of her thigh—a little too much of it.

They both looked down.

The condom had slid off.

Chapter Eight

Elena reached for a tissue from the box on the night-stand.

Rogan shook his head as his lips curved in a rueful smile. "My fault. I should have been more careful. Good thing you're on the pill."

"Yeah," she agreed as she wiped away the dribble of wetness. "Good thing." She wadded the tissue and tossed it into the wastebasket in the corner. Made it, too.

And it wasn't a big deal, she promised herself. She'd only messed up on that one pill, after all. And besides, it looked like the contents of the condom had spilled outside, not in.

"I'll be right back." He planted a quick kiss on the tip of her chin and rolled away from her.

When he returned from the bathroom, he reached for her hand. "All of a sudden, I'm starving."

"Me, too."

They got up, raided her freezer and stood in her kitchen naked eating Eskimo Pies. She laughed to think how quickly she was getting used to this, to being with him in this intimate way.

After the Eskimo Pies, they shared a bath. Her tub wasn't all that big, but they managed. He said it was cozy—and it certainly was.

Eventually, they went back to bed and made love again.

That second time was even better than the first. At the end, he rolled so she was on top. She folded her knees on either side of him and bent close, bracing her hands on the bed by his broad shoulders, letting her hair fall forward, a veil that hid them in their own secret world of sensation.

"This is…liberating," she whispered on a sharp hitch of breath.

Rogan's eyes were as soft as a swatch of green velvet. He reached up, threaded his fingers into her hair, brought her face down to within an inch of his. "You set the pace." He captured her mouth.

And she did set the pace. It was pure heaven. She never wanted it to end.

Too soon, she felt her body rising to the peak. She went with it, up and over the edge of the world. He followed, taking hold of her hips, pressing her down firmly onto him.

And that time, he was careful to withdraw soon after and to hold the base of the condom in place when he pulled away.

She whispered, "Stay the night."

He kissed her, a brushing butterfly caress of a kiss. "I thought you'd never ask."

In the morning, he was so tender with her.

When she confessed she was a little sore, he got right

up—and made breakfast. French toast with bacon. It was excellent. He said that with three kids to raise, he either had to learn to cook or they all would have ended up living on Big Macs and Chicken McNuggets.

"Not that I don't love me a nice, juicy Big Mac," he said. "But it never hurts to have a little variety in the menu."

After breakfast, they parted. He had to meet Cormac. She went to the hospital to see her dad—and her mom, too, since Luz hardly left his side.

Javier was cranky. Even with no complications, recovering from a coronary and open heart surgery was not an easy job. He said his incision was driving him crazy and he was already sick of his hospital room.

Luz was patient and sweet to him. And more than once, he almost forgot how miserable he was, he got so absorbed in gazing dreamily at his newly-regained wife.

At around half past eleven, Elena said she had to get going.

"Going where?" her mother and dad asked in unison.

She told them that she had agreed to meet Davis for lunch.

"Good," said her father.

"I'm glad," said her mom.

She didn't mention that she would be with Rogan later. After all, it was her own private business, what she and Rogan shared. And since it had no potential to go anywhere beyond the week or two he remained in San Antonio, she'd decided to play it totally cool.

If anyone asked, she'd say that she and Rogan were seeing each other casually, but it was nothing serious, that neither of them was interested in a long-distance relationship. She wasn't even going to tell Mercy that she was sleeping with him, not until months from now, when he was out of her life and she could look back on this special time with tenderness and appreciation.

Okay, the thought that it would end—and end so soon—made her feel a little sad. But she was not going to dwell on that tiny ache in her heart. She was going to enjoy herself thoroughly.

She was not going to think about the end. She was going to live each moment to the fullest.

Davis was already waiting at a table when she got to the restaurant. He jumped up at the sight of her—which seemed way out of character. He was such a big man with a truly commanding presence. He always wore expensive suits and people seemed to notice him wherever he went.

The nervous smile he gave her touched her. He really did care. He wanted to make some kind of relationship with her.

And she realized she was ready, at last, to form some kind of connection with him.

He ushered her into the booth opposite him. The waitress came and took their order.

Elena sipped iced tea as they waited for the food. He asked her about her school, her students. He wanted to know if she was happy with her life.

"Yes," she told him. "Very happy. Truly."

The food came. They ate and talked some more. Mostly surface stuff. It was kind of awkward. A lot of long silences—and then they would end up both starting to talk at the same time.

"Go ahead," he would say.

"No. Really. You go ahead...."

When the bill came, she glanced at her watch. Forty-five minutes she'd been sitting there, opposite him. It had seemed longer. But in time, she knew they would become more comfortable with each other.

He walked her out to her car. "I hope we can have lunch again sometime."

She told him she would like that.

He seemed to hesitate. So she took the lead, bending forward, brushing a quick kiss on his cheek. "Thanks for the lunch."

"Ahem. Yes. I enjoyed it."

It was kind of cute, really, she thought. Big, overbearing Davis Bravo, clearing his throat and acting downright shy.

She got in the car and he stood there on the walk in front of the restaurant, waving as she drove away.

After that, there were errands to run. She bought groceries, took them home and put them away and was back at the hospital by four.

Her dad was napping and her mom signaled her out into the hallway where she wanted to know how it went with Davis. Elena gave her a quick report and her mom got all dewy-eyed and said how proud she was of her.

They went back in the room where her dad was still sleeping. She'd just taken the chair next to her mom and turned on her ebook reader when her phone started vibrating. It was Rogan.

She slipped out to take the call.

"Tonight," he said, and a fine shiver of excitement went through her.

"Seven. My house. I'll cook."

"I'll be there."

She said goodbye and went back in the hospital room. Her mom gave her the *who was that?* look. Elena shrugged, leaned close and whispered, "A friend."

"What friend?"

"Just a friend." Elena picked up her ebook reader again, sat down and read a few chapters of the mystery she'd started a few nights and a lifetime ago, before her dad's heart attack.

Javier woke up at around five. A nurse came in to check his tubes and incision site. After that, they were bringing dinner in.

Elena kissed him, said she'd be back tomorrow and left him to her mom's loving care.

At home, she put a roast in the oven and set the table. Then she grabbed a quick shower before putting the potatoes on and cutting up the salad.

Rogan arrived right on time, with an armful of daylilies and a bottle of wine. She managed to get the flowers into a vase of water before he started kissing her.

And she kissed him back. Was there any activity on earth as satisfying as kissing Rogan?

Only making love with Rogan.

Which she did, before dinner. On the sofa in the living area. It was quick and thrilling—interrupted only by the necessity for her to run into the bedroom and grab a condom from the drawer by the bed.

The roast turned out well, she thought. And the wine he'd brought was delicious.

They went to bed early and made love for hours.

In the morning, they went out to breakfast, parted and met again in the evening to spend the night in each other's arms.

The next week school was out, so Elena was free to be with Rogan often and also to spend lots of time with her dad and mom.

Monday morning, over breakfast, she and Rogan decided they would keep their time together separate from any family gatherings. It was just better, easier, that way.

Elena loved her family so much. But she didn't need them all asking questions or developing…expectations. And if they saw her with Rogan, they were bound to get the picture that something really good was going on.

Because it was.

But it was also temporary. Her family might or might not understand that part. Whatever. It just wasn't their business.

Monday, Javier was released from the hospital. He went home with Luz and she made arrangements for all of his belongings to be moved out of his apartment and into the house they had decided to share.

Mercy and Luke came over. Luz made dinner for everyone. They all left early. Javier needed his rest.

Elena hurried to Rogan's waiting arms.

Tuesday, Wednesday and Thursday were pretty much the same. Days with the family. Nights in Rogan's arms.

Thursday night in bed after tender lovemaking, Rogan told her that he, Cormac, her dad and her mom were all meeting with the lawyers the next day to finalize the sale of Cabrera Construction to Murdoch Homes.

One week. She'd had exactly seven days with him. And now, already, it was ending.

She reminded herself that it was exactly as it should be. That she had made an agreement with him. And when he left, she would let him go with a smile on her face. "Congratulations."

He made a low sound in his throat and tightened his arm around her. His lips brushed against her temple and she thought how much she would miss him. Too much. It hurt just to think about it.

"Thanks. I'm really happy with the deal we've made." He kissed her temple again. "I think your dad is, too. He's built a great company over the years. We feel justified in meeting his price."

She ran her hand across the hard, warm flesh of his big chest and tried not to think about how much she was going to miss him. "So you'll be heading back to Dallas pretty soon, then." She was proud of how easy and accepting she sounded.

"Cormac's going back after the papers are signed."

"Tomorrow?"

"That's his plan."

"And you?" She spoke without looking up at him, her head on his shoulder, her gaze on the far wall. It seemed safer that way.

But he didn't allow her to avoid his eyes. He tipped her chin up. "I was thinking, if you can stand having me around a little longer, I would at least stay the weekend."

The weekend. Two whole days more. In an instant, her foolish heart turned from a ball of lead to a moonbeam. "I think I can put up with you...."

"I was hoping you would say that." He kissed her.

She gloried in that kiss.

And then he eased her over to lie on her back and kissed his way downward, lingering on her breasts, her belly....

By the time he reached his goal, she was more than ready for him. "So wet," he said, parting her, kissing her. "You are amazing..."

She reached out and grabbed the condom from where she'd left it by the lamp. Soon the world flew away. There was only his kiss, his knowing hands, the warmth of his breath against her most secret places.

Finally, she quivered and cried out.

And not long after that, she sat up and pushed him down to the pillows. She hitched a leg across him.

He said her name, his voice like rough velvet.

She gazed down at him, enjoying the power she had over him, admiring the way he curved up so hard and ready, eager for her, from the nest of dark brown hair at the top of his powerful thighs. "You're always so happy to see me...."

"You know I am." He growled the words. It was a hungry sort of growl.

She bent over him, stuck out her tongue and tasted him. He moaned. She smiled as she lowered her mouth onto him. He moaned some more.

She took him right to the edge.

And then, with a swiftness and dexterity that she never would have dreamed of a week ago, she tore the top off the foil pouch and rolled it expertly down over him. She rose up on her knees and slowly, by careful degrees, lowered her body onto his.

After that, it was fast and wild and wonderful. They climbed to the peak together and finished almost as one.

A little later, when he pulled the covers up over them and whispered good-night, she cuddled in close to him and tried not to imagine all the ways she might be able to convince him to stay with her, all the sensual enticements she had at her disposal now, to help hold him to her, to make him realize that being single and unencumbered wouldn't be all that great, after all.

Friday, Saturday, Sunday...

Three more days to be with him. She was going to treasure every minute they had left.

But the minutes flew by. The hours refused to slow.

Too soon, it was Sunday.

They spent the day together, wandering the River Walk, stopping for lunch there and then going back to her condo in the afternoon, making slow, lazy love.

Later, they got up and she made them dinner. They went back to bed. Their lovemaking was more frantic, then. Three times, he took her to the brink and over.

Neither of them could get enough of touching each other, of loving each other. Their time, after all, was ending.

He was driving back home in the morning.

They were up before dawn. She had school that day. He made her favorite breakfast—French toast with bacon.

As they were clearing the table, he caught her arm. He gathered her close. He kissed her, a deep kiss. And then he took her face between his cherishing hands. "I've been thinking...."

She tried a laugh. "Uh-oh."

"I could come down next weekend. We could be together."

Her heart did a forward roll. He didn't want it to end any more than she did. That meant a lot.

So very much.

But she caught his wrists, wrapped her smaller hands around his big ones, pressed them together. "Are you saying that maybe the freedom you've been dreaming of isn't all that important, after all?"

His gaze slid away. "I just don't want to lose you."

She knew then. He wanted her. But he hadn't given up his longing to have a life on his own. He still wanted that most of all.

And she had made him a promise. A good promise. A fair one. He had given her so much, introduced her to a side of herself she'd been longing to meet.

But the time had come to let him go.

She went on tiptoe, kissed him. "I think it's better if we call an end now. That was the agreement and it works best for me."

He caught her face in his hands again. "God. I am going to miss you."

"I'll miss you, too. But it's the best way."

He didn't argue.

A little while later, he got his things together—his razor, shaving cream and aftershave from her bathroom, a few random items of clothing from the dresser drawer she'd given him to use when he stayed with her, his light jacket from the entry closet.

He kissed her at the door. A lingering kiss.

When he lifted his head, she gave him a slow smile. "Goodbye, Rogan. Have an absolutely terrific life."

He didn't say anything. Just pulled open the door and went out.

She shut it quickly after him.

She couldn't bear to watch him go.

Chapter Nine

Five months later: October.

Elena opened the door. The fall evening was cool and pleasant.

The expression on her brother's face? Not so much.

"What now?" she asked, feeling tired and grim and hating that she knew what was coming.

"I just wanted to see how you were doing, that's all."

Her hand instinctively went to her belly. Protectively, she curved her fingers over the growing roundness there. She said, "Caleb." Just that, just his name, with a weariness bordering on resignation. And then, softly, "Don't, okay? Let's not do this. I love you. You know that. But I don't want to talk about it. I've said all I'm going to say on the subject."

"How about a cup of coffee?"

"You're not going to get me to say any more."

"About what?"

She blew out a breath. He knew very well what. "Go home."

He didn't budge. "Just some coffee. Come on."

She heaved a sigh. They couldn't stand out here on her front step forever. It was either let him in or shut the door in his face.

Reluctantly, she let him in.

He followed her to the kitchen, where he sat at the counter as she poured water into the coffeemaker, stuck a filter in the basket and spooned in the French roast. She hit the brew button, turned and faced him. "Ready in a few minutes."

"Great. Thanks."

They stared at each other. As a top notch salesman, Caleb knew a hundred ways to dominate an argument. One was to get the other person to be the one to mention a disputed issue first.

But he was out of luck this time. She knew that trick and she wasn't going to fall for it.

Behind her, the brew cycle started with a hiss, followed by a slow trickling sound.

Finally, Caleb gave in and spoke. "So. You're feeling good?"

"Yes, I am. Thanks."

"I talked to Rogan today."

Apprehension slithered through her. She resisted the desire to fold her arms across her big stomach, a gesture of self-protection that Caleb would instantly recognize. No weakness, she reminded herself. He thinks he knows.

But he doesn't know.

She said lightly, "Oh? How's he doing?"

"He asked me how *you* were."

"No kidding? And what did you tell him?"

Caleb's pleasant expression had faded. He gave up hiding

his real agenda. Now, he seethed where he sat. "Nothing. I said you were fine. I kept my damn word to you, didn't mention that you just happen to be five months along."

"And why would you mention that, Caleb? Since I asked you not to, since I told you to please, *please* mind your own business."

"Why would you care if Rogan Murdoch knows that you're having a baby?"

"I told you. I hardly know the guy," she baldly lied. "And that means it's none of his business, either. Even less so than it is yours, actually."

"Why would you want to keep it a secret from him— unless he's the father and you're afraid to tell him?"

"Secret? It's not a secret. It's just not your place to go around telling a bunch of near-strangers that I'm having a baby and you want to know who the dad is."

"I wouldn't call Rogan a near-stranger."

"Of course you wouldn't. You've known him for years. I haven't."

"He's a good man. You have to know that he'll step up, as soon as he knows what's going on."

Yeah. She knew. And the thought of Rogan's stepping up, of knowing that he would because that was who he was—that broke her heart.

"Butt out," she told Caleb.

And yes, she did plan to tell Rogan. But not on Caleb's schedule, thank you very much.

She would tell Rogan as soon as the baby was born. She felt so terrible about the whole thing. And she considered it the least she could do for her baby's father, to honor the promise she'd made him, the promise she knew she was eventually going to have to break. The promise to let him go, let him have the freedom he craved.

Yes, he had a right to know he had a child.

But Rogan didn't have a child *yet*. And there was no reason he had to know about the baby for months. Not until their son was born—and yes, according to the ultrasound she'd had two weeks ago, her baby was a boy.

Caleb stared at her through narrowed eyes. "*I know*, Elena. There's no doubt in my mind. Rogan's the one."

A shiver went through her and her mouth went dry.

But uh-uh. Caleb didn't really know, she reminded herself for the umpteenth time. Not for certain. He was only faking her out, trying to get her to bust to the truth.

He felt guilty. She got that. Because Rogan was *his* friend. Because if it hadn't been for him hooking Rogan up with her dad, she never would have met the man.

"Nice try," she said, ladling on the sarcasm. "You know nothing of the kind."

"I do know," he insisted. "I know you went out with him at least once. And I saw the way you looked at each other, Easter Sunday, out at the ranch, the way you stuck close together all afternoon, like neither of you could stand being out of the other's sight. I even saw you holding hands. And I've talked to Antonio. He says he never—"

"You *what?*"

Caleb scowled—and his Adam's apple bounced up and down as he gulped. He knew damn well he'd finally gone too far. "Look. If it *was* Antonio, I think he would want to know."

"That does it." She slapped a hand down on the counter between them.

"Elena, come on…"

"Out."

Now he actually looked worried. "Elena, I didn't get into it with Antonio. Seriously. He said he never did more than kiss you. And I believe that. I—"

"*Out*, Caleb. Out of my house. Now."

"But if you would only—"

"Out." She did fold her hands over her round belly then. She folded them and she pinned him with her most unforgiving, unwavering stare.

He got up from the stool. "Look, I really—"

"Out."

His big shoulders slumped. "Okay. I'm sorry. I shouldn't have—"

"No. You shouldn't. You had no right to go bothering Tonio. None. And I am furious with you, Caleb. I want you to leave and I want you to leave now."

He finally got the message. Carefully pushing the stool under the lip of the counter, he turned for the door.

She didn't see him out, didn't even breathe until she heard the door click shut behind him.

And then she sagged against the counter, braced her elbows on the cool granite and put her head in her hands. What was she going to do about him? He was obsessed with finding out who her baby's father was—or rather, with getting her to admit that it was Rogan.

Maybe she ought to call Irina about him, see if his levelheaded wife could talk a little sense into that thick head of his—not that she cared right then. Right then, she was thinking that she might never speak to him again.

Behind her, on the sink counter, the coffeemaker beeped.

She whirled, grabbed the carafe and poured the steaming contents down the drain.

Two months later: December.

Caleb stood on her doorstep, arms full of brightly wrapped Christmas presents. "I can't stand this. I'm sorry. You know I am. And this is stupid. You can't keep running into me at family get-togethers and pretending I'm not even there."

Her heart melted. But she refused to show it. "Hah. Watch me."

"Elena, hey. Give it up. I'm your favorite brother, remember? You have to speak to me eventually."

Okay, he was right. She couldn't go on like this. He'd been a complete ass about the whole thing. But she loved him. So much. She missed hanging out with him and Irina. Yes, she still got to visit with Irina at family gatherings. And she got to hold their sweet baby, Hanna, born in August, now and then.

But it wasn't the same as having them come to her place. Or going to their house and chowing down on Irina's amazing cooking.

And two months was probably long enough to punish him for being beyond pushy and butting into her private business, for going after poor Antonio who didn't have a thing to do with any of this. Who had a right to live his life with his darling Tappy and not be confronted by some old girlfriend's overprotective big brother.

"Elena," Caleb pleaded. "Come on. Friends?"

"Will you leave it alone, then? Stay out of it? Please?"

"I swear. It's your business. I understand that now." He looked so contrite.

She couldn't stand being mad at him. Not for another second more. "All right. Come on in."

His face broke into a wide, relieved smile. "Finally."

Inside, he went straight for the living room and the tree in front of the window that faced the side balcony. "Nice tree." He knelt to put the armful of gifts under it.

She stood over him, her stomach a lot bigger than it had been when she'd kicked him out two months before, her hands at her lower back, rubbing the achy spot there. "Want some coffee?"

Still kneeling, he beamed up at her. "I thought you'd never ask."

She made him some coffee and turned on the tree lights and they sat in the living room, talking and laughing together, pretty much like old times. He never once mentioned Rogan or the ongoing mystery of who her baby's father might be.

She told herself to be grateful for small favors, for brief reprieves.

Truth was, she might have told him that he was right about Rogan. If she only could have trusted him to keep it to himself.

A month before, she'd told her sister and her mom and dad that Rogan was the baby's father. They'd all promised to tell no one. To stay out of it. Even her dad. But then, Javier had learned a lot when he went into counseling for his anger issues. He only insisted that once the baby was born, Rogan would have to know.

And she had promised him that Rogan *would* know.

It wouldn't be long now. A couple of months and she would be keeping her promise.

Oh, she dreaded that.

So she'd decided she was going to stop thinking about it. She would enjoy the holidays, finish getting ready for the baby.

And she would worry about telling Rogan later. She would try not to even think about it until the time came.

Two months later, February 10th.

"Pass those potatoes over here," Elena demanded.

Irina handed her the bowl. Elena ladled a giant scoop

onto her plate. So what if she didn't have a prayer of eating more than a few bites now the baby had pushed most of her digestive system up against her breastbone. Irina made the best garlic potatoes in the world.

Caleb was watching her, looking vaguely perplexed. "How late are you, anyway?"

"Exactly a week." She took the bowl of steamed asparagus and carefully transferred a nice, big helping to her plate next to the large mound of potatoes.

"Is everything all right?" He frowned.

Elena and Irina shared a glance of womanly wisdom and mutual understanding.

Then Irina said, "First babies are often late. You know that, Caleb. We read about that in the baby books before Hanna was born."

"Uh. We did? Hanna was right on time, born on her due date."

"Lucky you," said Elena mildly as she piled on a couple of thick slices of perfectly roasted pork shoulder. She passed the platter on to her brother and picked up her fork and knife.

Caleb shook his head as he served himself. "Well, I'm getting worried. That baby better come soon."

His wife reached over, patted his arm. "A week late is nothing to get concerned about."

"That's right. Everything's fine." Elena sliced off a tender bite of meat and dredged it in the amazing potatoes. She put the bite in her mouth and chewed. "Heaven, Irina. As always."

Irina smiled modestly. "I am so glad you like it."

"You are the best cook in the whole world. Just another reason I'm glad you married my annoying big brother."

"Hey." Caleb pretended to look hurt. "You couldn't get along without me."

"True. But that doesn't make you any less aggravating." She ate another bite of potatoes and sighed in pleasure at the taste.

The last few weeks, Irina was constantly inviting her over to eat. Elena really appreciated the great meals and the good company. Plus, since they'd had Hanna, her brother and sister-in-law had started eating dinner early. No more cocktails at seven and dinner at eight.

They ate at six, sometimes even earlier, which suited Elena perfectly. Lately, by nine, she was ready for bed.

Elena picked up her water glass. She set it back on the table without drinking from it when she felt the funniest little twinge, low down. "Ouch."

Caleb stiffened. "What? Is it—?"

Elena and Irina laughed in unison and Elena said, "Settle down, big brother. It's nothing. Just a cramp."

But an hour and a half later, the cramps were starting to get stronger. And she found herself timing them as she sat in one of the big lounge chairs in Caleb and Irina's media room watching some thriller Caleb had chosen.

She waited until the end of the chase scene, when the main characters were in a dark warehouse trying to decide what to do next, before admitting, "Sorry, guys. I think I need to call my doctor."

The doctor said she would meet Elena at the hospital.

Everything was ready to go. Elena was pre-admitted. And she called her mom and dad and her sister before they left Caleb's house.

Luz would go straight to the hospital and meet her there. Javier would stop off at the condo to pick up the fully-packed suitcase waiting in the coat closet by the front door. Mercy was on her way, too. It would take her a little longer, coming in from the ranch. And she wanted to feed her baby daughter, two-month-old Serena, before she left.

"But I'll be there as quick as I can, *chica*," she vowed.

Irina stayed home with the sleeping Hanna. Caleb drove Elena to the hospital in his prized Audi R8—the new one he'd bought to replace the one he'd wrecked a couple of years ago.

He hustled her out to the car and they took off. Literally. He drove way too fast. But then, he always had.

Elena tried to ignore the speedometer and the sounds of the tires squealing. It wasn't that hard. She had plenty to do just riding out her contractions, gripping the armrest to steady herself when the pain got too bad.

At the hospital—Sisters of Mercy, the same hospital where her father had had open heart surgery last year—Caleb pulled in beneath the maternity wing's porte cochere.

She sent him a grateful smile. "Thanks, big brother."

"I'll park and come in."

"Great." She popped the clasp on her seat belt and reached for the door latch.

He grabbed her arm before she could shove the door open.

She frowned at him. "Caleb, what in the…?"

His expression was way too intent. "I know that he would want to know, want to be here. I think you know it, too."

Suddenly, she wanted to burst into tears. Or maybe bop her brother on the head with her purse. "Caleb. Come on. Can't you see I'm a little busy right now?"

He refused to let go of her arm. "Let me call him. Before it's too late…"

"Caleb, you promised."

He continued as if she'd never spoken. "Before his son is born without him there to see it. A man has a right to be there, to see his baby born."

"Oh, God…" Another contraction started. She sat there in that gorgeous car, panting, riding it out. When it was over, she realized that Caleb had given her his hand to hold onto.

"Okay?" he asked, so gently.

She couldn't tell if he meant was *she* okay? Or was it okay if he called Rogan?

Maybe a little of both.

She sucked in a slow breath. "I need to go in."

"I know. I'll help you. Screw it. I can leave the car here."

"No, really, I…" Right then, she glanced toward the building and saw Luz coming out through the two sets of double doors. She followed an orderly pushing a wheelchair. "My mom's here. She can take me in."

"Great, then. That's handled. Let me call Rogan."

She wanted to punch his lights out. But he did have a point. Rogan might want to be there for the birth. "All right."

Caleb smiled then. "Good."

And instantly she realized what a bad idea that was, what a terrible thing to do to Rogan, to let Caleb call him, out of the blue with the big news that she was not only having his baby, she was having his baby *now*.

Uh-uh. Bad, bad idea. She needed to wait, as she'd always planned to do, to call him after the baby was born, when she was able to think more rationally. She needed to tell him herself, not hide behind her brother. "Wait. No. Never mind. This isn't the right time."

"Elena, it's never going to feel like the right time."

She wanted to cry again. "It's really rotten of you to do this when you swore you wouldn't—especially now, when I can't even think." There was a tap on her side window.

Her mom. She rolled the window down. "Just a minute, okay?"

Luz and the orderly blinked in unison and her mom said, "*M'hija*, come on, now. The doctor's waiting."

"All right, all right." She pushed open the door and swung her feet to the pavement, pausing before she turned and settled into the wheelchair to mutter over her shoulder, "Caleb. Don't."

"It's the best thing. You know it." He was still smiling. "Don't worry, little sister. It's all going to work out just fine."

Chapter Ten

"Oh, Rogan." His date laughed at the silly joke he'd just made. She had a great laugh, really. Kind of husky. "I'm so glad we're doing this." Her name was Pauline Trent and she was a nice woman. She owned a coffee bar, Perfect Brew, where he'd been buying his morning coffee since Brenda went off to school in New York.

"I'm glad, too." His cell vibrated in his breast pocket. He tried to ignore it. "What do you think? Ready to look at the dessert menu?"

"Oh, I don't know…"

"Come on. Take a chance. We can split something."

She slanted him a glance. "I can hear that thing buzzing."

He gave her a rueful smile. "And they call it 'silent page.'"

"It's okay. Really. Go ahead and answer it."

He pulled the phone out, though by then the vibrating had stopped.

You have 2 missed calls.

Caleb. Again. He'd called once already, about a half an hour ago. Rogan had felt fine about letting the first call go to voice mail to deal with later. But this second call worried him. Was there some emergency?

Another message popped onto the screen: *You have 2 voice mails.*

He thought, *Elena. Could something have happened to Elena?*

And then he told himself not to be an idiot. Caleb didn't even know about him and Elena. If she was sick or in trouble, Caleb would hardly be calling him.

Unless, maybe, she had asked for him....

"You should see your face," Pauline said.

He looked up from the phone, tried to smile.

"Go ahead," she said. "Call whoever it is back. I'll get us something chocolate." She signaled for the waiter.

"Two spoons?"

"You got it."

He rose, dropped his napkin on the chair and headed for the hallway outside the restrooms. There were pay phones there. And stools. He took one of the stools and hit the call back button on his cell.

Caleb answered before Rogan even heard a ring on the other end. "There you are. About time." He sounded frazzled. Annoyed. Maybe angry, even.

"Caleb, what's going on?"

"You sitting down?"

"You're scaring the crap out of me. What?"

"It's Elena."

He realized Caleb had been right to ask if he was sitting

down. He felt suddenly disconnected from his legs and his feet. "My God. What?"

"You really thought I didn't have a clue, huh? My sister, you sonofabitch. My *innocent* sister—and don't you try and tell me she wasn't. I know her, I know what she meant when she used to joke about being *too* good of a Catholic girl...."

So. All right. That was the issue here. Caleb knew. And he was seriously pissed.

Rogan could understand that. "She didn't want you to know about us, okay? That was her choice. And if you just have to beat my face in over this, we can arrange for that. Later. Right now, I'm—"

"You get down here. You get on a plane and you get your ass to SA."

He didn't argue. It was only fair. "I will. Tomorrow morning, first thing."

"Not tomorrow. Now. Tonight."

Rogan blew out a slow breath. "Caleb, I can't manage it tonight."

"You can't manage it." Each word dripped disgust.

"No. I'm sorry, but I can't."

"Are you listening? Sisters of Mercy Hospital. Got that?"

His heart bounced into his throat. She was in the hospital for some reason? "What are you saying? Is she—?"

"Let me put it this way. If you want to be here to see your son born, you'd better get here tonight."

At the table, Pauline was eating a miniature chocolate cake, one with fudge sauce pooling beneath it. She set down her spoon when she saw his face. "An emergency?"

"Sorry. We have to go."

He took Pauline home. Twice, the poor woman asked him to slow down. He didn't.

At her house, she jumped right out. "Call me. Let me know...."

He knew he wouldn't be calling her. So he only said, "Goodbye, Pauline. I'm really sorry about this." Sorry didn't begin to cover it. He was feeling like a total douche on so many levels.

She ran up the front steps and let herself in. He put it in gear and peeled rubber out of there, headed straight for the airport.

By some minor miracle, he got a seat on a ten-thirty flight, the last flight to San Antonio that night. The flight took an hour. It only seemed like a lifetime.

Pregnant.

Elena got pregnant.

He couldn't believe it. She'd been on the pill. They'd used condoms faithfully. Even with that one slipping off that first time, well, it shouldn't have happened.

But it had. He knew her well enough to know that she wouldn't be saying he was the father if it wasn't true.

A baby. She was having his baby. Rogan felt something like wonder.

He also felt a slow anger, like hot coals burning red beneath a layer of ash. All those times he'd almost called her—but stopped himself before he actually went through with it. He *should* have called her. Maybe if he had, she would have busted to the truth before now.

Maybe if he had, he wouldn't be racing against the clock to have a prayer of being there when his own child was born.

Or maybe not.

Did she think she could have his baby and not even tell

him? Just because they'd agreed to end it for good back in May?

That was low. She had to know that all agreements were off once a kid was involved.

He called Caleb again while he was waiting at the rental kiosk for a car. "You said it was a boy."

"That's right. She had one of those routine ultrasounds several months ago."

"Well, then. Is my son born yet?"

"Where are you?"

"Here, in San Antonio. At the airport. Waiting for a car."

Grudgingly, Caleb admitted, "She's still in labor."

"I'm on my way."

"How long?"

"Half an hour."

"I'll be waiting under the porte cochere in front of the maternity wing."

Caleb was there, sitting on a bench outside the twin sets of double glass doors, as promised. When Rogan pulled in, he got up and ran around to the driver's side.

Rogan pushed open his door. "How is she?"

"They took her to the delivery room. It won't be long now. I told them that the father was on his way. They're waiting for you. They'll take you in—so you can be there for the birth."

Suddenly, his brain seemed to have gone on hold. He just sat in the rental car with the door wide open, feeling poleaxed.

Caleb said, "Wake up. Get out."

He shook himself. "I need to park...."

"No time. Go on in. I'll deal with the car."

So Rogan got out. He was half expecting Caleb to punch

him a good one, right there in front of the maternity wing. But he didn't. He just got in the car, pulled the door shut and drove away.

Moving on autopilot, sure this must be some weird, impossible dream he was having, Rogan turned and approached the glass doors.

Inside, he saw Javier sitting in the waiting room, looking a damn sight healthier than he had nine months ago, but also very serious. Downright somber. Luke Bravo was there, too. Which meant that Luz and Mercy were probably in with Elena.

The men rose and came to him. Were they as pissed at him as Caleb was? Apparently not quite. They didn't smile. But they each shook his hand.

Luke said, "Glad you made it," and sounded as though he meant it.

Javier clapped him on the back—a gesture that might have meant just about anything.

A woman in scrubs on the other side of the admissions desk asked, "Mr. Murdoch?"

"That's me."

"Let's get you a gown…."

At first, Elena didn't know that Rogan had come into the birthing room.

She was out of transition by then, right on past what they called active labor and on to the pushing part. Or she would be, if only her doctor would give her the go-ahead on that.

Her mom was on one side of her and Mercy on the other and her OB-GYN, Dr. Amina Sankay, was down there between her legs. The lights were low and everyone was trying to be really peaceful, really soothing.

Gentle hands touched her, stroked the sweaty side of

her neck, rubbed her shoulder and her upper back. Gentle voices told her to breathe. And she was in a world of pain and wanting so bad to push and push until she had her son safely born and held him close in her waiting arms.

But Dr. Sankay kept telling her, "Not yet. Don't push yet…."

And she groaned and told them all, "I have to. I can't stand it."

Her mom said, "No, *m'hija*. Not yet. Listen to your doctor. Wait. Not yet…"

And she tossed the sweaty, stringy hair out of her eyes, gritted her teeth so hard she was lucky they didn't crack, and moaned long and loud at the ceiling. It was an awful sound, like the moo of a foundering cow. If she'd had any dignity left, she would have been humiliated that such a sound was coming from her own mouth.

But by then, all her modesty was long gone. She didn't care what she sounded like—or what she looked like. She just wanted to push.

But once more, her doctor said, "Not yet. Soon…"

And she mooed like a cow again. And right then, as the long, ridiculous groan faded off and she lowered her head, she just happened to glance toward the door.

Rogan was standing there in a blue hospital gown.

"Rogan?" she croaked in complete disbelief. And then she groaned again—a groan that had nothing to do with the pain she was feeling.

Rogan. By the door. Was she having hallucinations?

She blinked.

But when she looked again, he was still there. He moved closer.

And then Mercy said quietly, "Rogan. Good to see you." Which confirmed it. He was actually there. Mercy even tipped her head at him, signaling him closer still as she scooted toward the headrail, clearing him a spot at the bedside.

He took that spot, looming large right beside her. Somehow, she couldn't quite look in his face. She stared at the front of his wrinkled blue gown. She didn't know what she felt right then, beyond the pain of her baby trying to be born. This wasn't how she'd planned for him to meet his son.

But evidently, this was how it was going to happen.

And that he had dropped everything and caught a flight to get here—well, that was probably a good sign, wasn't it?

She gathered her courage and lifted her gaze to meet those clover-green eyes. "So." She was panting, *willing* the next contraction to wait for a moment. "Caleb called you...."

He nodded, but he didn't say anything.

And then Mercy surrendered Elena's hand to him. He wrapped his big fingers around it. And she felt a sudden... lifting. As if he'd reached over and taken away a weight, a burden she hadn't even realized she was carrying.

And all at once, she was glad—so glad. That he was here.

Glad enough that she wasn't even mad at Caleb anymore for going against her final, frantic instructions and calling him anyway.

With her hand clasped firmly in his, Rogan spoke at last. He said pretty much what Caleb had said, when he let her out of the car in front of the maternity wing, "Don't worry about anything. Everything will work out fine."

Did she believe him?

Not really.

Still, it was absolutely the right thing for him to say at that moment. It was what she needed to hear. Oh, they had so much to talk about, she and Rogan. Too much. Difficult things were going to have to be said. He had to be wondering how she could possibly be having his baby, given that she'd said she was on the pill.

Not to mention, they'd been extra careful and used condoms, too.

But at least he didn't seem to doubt that it was *his* baby.

And right now, well, she had a job to do. A job that wasn't going to wait for the two of them to talk.

And then Dr. Sankay said, "All right, now. It's time. Push when you feel like it, Elena. You go ahead and you push."

And she did. She closed her eyes and shut Rogan out—shut everything out. Everything but the baby that was coming, everything but her body's need to make that happen.

Now, at least, when the contractions came, she was past being so exhausted she could hardly go on. She had her second wind. She panted and she screamed some more. She mooed like a big old cow.

And she pushed.

Her hair was soaking wet and her face was dripping sweat and her legs were spread wide open for everyone to see. Everybody was speaking in low voices, saying how great she was doing as she held on to Rogan's big hand and she yelled and pushed and felt as if she could absolutely do this one second—and as if she would split right down the middle the next.

And then the baby's head crowned. And Elena kept on screaming and Dr. Sankay said to keep pushing.

And she did.

And then, as she screamed and panted, the doctor said, "The shoulders, we've got the shoulders. Yes. There we go...."

And that was it. Her baby slithered the rest of the way out without any more effort on her part.

Dr. Sankay caught him. He let out a loud, furious cry. Elena glanced over at the clock on the wall.

1:32 in the morning. February 11th. The day her son was born.

A day that would be precious to her for the rest of her life.

"A big, gorgeous boy," said the doctor.

"Oh, he's a healthy one," said her mother. "You can tell by the way he cries."

"Beautiful," Mercy said.

He wasn't. Not really. He had puffy red eyes and his head was kind of cone-shaped, like Elena had read it might be at first, from pushing through the birth canal. Plus, in the folds of his skin, he had bits of what they called Vernix caseosa, a yucky curdled-looking yellowish substance that she'd read was supposed to have protected him against the amniotic fluid in the womb.

But he was certainly big and he had big hands for a newborn, hands balled into fists, waving, air boxing as he sucked in another breath and wailed some more.

She loved him on sight. Who wouldn't? She reached out for him. "Please. I need to hold him."

"Of course you do." Dr. Sankay gave him to her, laid him on her belly, with the umbilical cord still attached.

He quieted instantly. And she cried then, the tears dripping down over her temples, into her already sweat-soaked hair.

"You're here," she whispered to him, her baby, her little boy, as she curved a cherishing hand around his nearly-bald, funny-shaped head. "I'm so glad you're here."

Rogan leaned close. She felt his warmth, felt his breath brush her temple. He touched the baby's hand and instantly, the red fist opened, grasping, the small fingers wrapping around Rogan's larger one.

"I'd like to name him Michael," Rogan said. "After my dad. If that's all right with you?"

Again, she found it hard to look at him. It seemed so strange, that he was here, now, after all these months and months when he hadn't been—not that she had a problem with his being here.

It was right that he was here. She knew that.

Right, but very strange.

Still, somehow, through the tears that clogged her throat, she managed to whisper, "Michael is a beautiful name. It will do just fine. I want his middle name to be Javier."

"Michael Javier it is."

Chapter Eleven

Two hours later, Elena's mom and dad, her sister and Luke and Caleb, too, had gone on home to get some much-needed rest.

The nurses settled her and Michael into a room. The room had two beds, but no privacy curtains, which seemed odd to Elena. Would she be sharing an open room with a stranger and another baby?

"For the baby's father," the nurse said, when she saw Elena eyeing that empty bed. "Your husband said to tell you he'll be back soon. He had to run out to the drugstore, to pick up a few things."

He's not my husband, Elena thought, though she didn't actually say it out loud. Was he really going to sleep in here with her and the baby?

She didn't know if she was ready for that.

Back in May, when he'd left her, she'd felt as though she knew him so intimately, knew him as well as she knew the members of her own family. He was in her heart. In her mind. In her soul, a part of her.

Or at least, it had seemed that way then.

But now, after all these months without so much as a shared word between them...

She didn't know him anymore. If she ever really had. She was glad he had come in time to be there for his son's birth. But still, it made her uncomfortable to think of trying to sleep in the same room with him.

The nurse started explaining the hospital's rooming-in policy. "It's all right," she said, "if you want to keep your baby with you round-the-clock until your doctor releases you. But we are perfectly happy and ready to take him to the nursery anytime you feel too tired or need a break. He can stay with you however much you want. Or you can give him to us and get your rest."

At that moment, Michael happened to be sleeping like an angel. Elena touched the side of the bassinet, smiled tenderly down at his scrunched-up little face. "I'll ring for you if I need a break."

"Good then. You've already tried nursing him...."

She nodded. "I thought it went pretty well. And when he wakes up, I'm going to try it again."

"Don't overtax yourself."

"I won't. I promise."

The nurse slipped out, pausing to brace the door open a few inches behind her.

Elena turned off the light and lay there in the near-dark with her new baby sleeping beside her, wondering how long it would be before Rogan came back. She yawned.

Every muscle in her body ached. She hurt in places she'd never even known she *had* until now. And she was too tired to keep her eyes open.

Within minutes of the nurse's leaving, she was fast asleep.

* * *

Armed with a brown sack containing toothbrush, tooth-paste, shaving cream and razor, Rogan stuck his head in the partially-opened door of Elena's room.

It was dark in there.

And very quiet.

With care, so as not to disturb her or the baby, he flipped up the doorstop and eased the door wide enough that he could squeeze through. Then he let the door slide back to the way he'd found it and put the stop down again.

She was asleep. Michael was, too.

Standing there at the door, he could hear the sound of breathing—the woman's and the child's.

He bent and slipped off his shoes. In his stocking feet, he went into the bathroom and shut the door—slowly, so the latch didn't click. He washed his hands, splashed a little water on his face and brushed his teeth.

Then, leaving the bag and its contents behind in the bathroom, he turned off the light and crept back out into the main room.

The baby's bassinet was between Elena's bed and the empty one. He couldn't resist tiptoeing over there, getting another look at him.

Michael.

Even with the puffy eyes and that wrinkled, ancient newborn look, he was clearly a Murdoch. Big and healthy. Ready to take on the world.

Rogan's dad would have been so damn proud.

Unfair, that Michael Murdoch couldn't be here to see him. To hold his first grandson in his burly arms.

I'm here now, Michael, Rogan made the promise silently, in order not to wake the baby or the new mom. *Here for you. And your mother. You're safe. I will take care of you.*

The freedom he'd wanted so much?

Well, this was life, wasn't it? A man did what he had to do. And doing the right thing brought with it certain... rewards.

He glanced at the sleeping woman in the bed. Her head was turned away from him, the line of her jaw and her slim throat silvery in the darkness. He'd hated giving her up.

Now he wouldn't have to.

Life wasn't fair. But there were compensations.

Crying.

Someone was crying.

Elena forced her way up through the heavy layers of deep sleep.

The baby. *Michael.* His name was Michael.

And he was crying....

She opened her eyes and turned her head toward the bassinet.

Empty.

She gasped and popped to a sitting position, groaning as every one of her poor, abused muscles complained. "My baby..."

"Hey." A whispered voice in the darkness—Rogan. "It's okay. He's right here..." He came toward her out of the shadows, his steps silent in stocking feet. He had the fussing baby in his arms.

"Give him to me." She held out her hands.

Rogan passed him to her. She eased her gown out of the way and put him to her breast.

She'd read about how nursing took patience. That sometimes the baby wouldn't catch on right away. Michael had no such problem. He latched on and sucked greedily.

She smiled down at him and stroked his pointy head over the little baby cap the nurses had put on him. "Piece of cake, huh?" she whispered tenderly to him.

"He knows what's good for him," Rogan said. He was still standing above her. "A Murdoch, through and through."

She felt suddenly exposed and adjusted her gown a little, so that less of her breast was showing. And when she looked up, her gaze scooted past his. Out the high window on the other side of Rogan's bed, she saw that the sky was growing light. "What time is it?"

"Almost seven."

She looked down at her baby again. Amazing. Impossible. He was here, in her arms. At last.

"I was hoping to let you sleep a little longer," Rogan said.

It was getting ridiculous, that she didn't look at him. So she made herself do it. Even in the shadowed room, she thought he looked tired. "Go on back to bed."

He seemed to search her face. What did he see? Stringy hair and baggy eyes? Or maybe her guilt about this whole situation? He said, "I don't mind taking him. As soon as he's…done."

She shook her head. "I think he'll go to sleep again. It's fine. That's what they do, isn't it? Cry. Nurse. Sleep."

He didn't say anything. He just went on looking at her. She wondered what he was thinking, but decided it probably wasn't that good of an idea to ask.

Yes, they needed to talk.

But not right now. *Please. Not right now.*

Finally, he said, "Well, all right then. I'm here, if you need me."

Yeah, and where were you for the past nine months?

The angry words just popped into her mind. But she didn't say them. They were unfair, and she knew it. How could he possibly have been here, given that she hadn't bothered to tell him she needed him?

She had to remember that she had willingly agreed to

the terms for what they'd shared, that he never would have been her lover in the first place if she hadn't sworn she would let him go.

Madre de Dios. It was all a big mess and she couldn't think about it right now.

He turned from her and went to the other bed and stretched out on it, still wearing all of his clothes, turning on his side to face the window—away from her.

Which was good. Great. Michael pulled off the breast and started fussing a little. She switched him to the other side and he went right to work. He wasn't getting food right now, she knew that. Her milk wouldn't come down for a few days. But apparently, he found the act of nursing comforting. A few minutes on that breast and he was asleep again.

Carefully, she tucked him into his bassinet. He didn't wake.

So she turned over on her side—away from the baby and from the man in the other bed—and shut her eyes.

Sleep settled over her.

The next time she woke, brighter light slanted in the window—but the clock on the wall said it was only an hour later. Someone had brought in a breakfast tray for her—and one for Rogan, too. He was sitting up, eating from his tray one-handed, holding Michael on his other arm.

He gave her a smile. "Hungry?"

"I think I want a shower."

"Need some help?"

Not on your life. "No, thanks. I can manage." Stifling a groan, she pushed back the covers and swung her bare feet to the floor.

The shower felt wonderful. But by the time she got dried off, put on a fresh pad and clean underwear and got back into her nightgown, she was too exhausted to bother blow-drying her hair.

The mirror over the sink told a sad, sad story. Limp, stringy wet hair. Purple bruises under her eyes. Her skin looked slick and pasty. Ugh.

She towel-dried her hair as best she could and trudged back into the main room.

"I was starting to worry you had drowned," Rogan teased. He'd finished his food and put Michael back down.

"It was very refreshing," she said wryly. "Now I only need to sleep for a week."

"Sleep as long as you like. I'm here."

He'd said that before, *I'm here*. What did that mean? How long was he staying?

She should ask, but if she asked then they would be having *the talk*. And she wanted to avoid that for as long as possible.

Really, she was a total coward. And right now, she was just too tired to care.

The bed was harder to get into than it had been to get out of. But she managed it. And then she forced herself to eat a little of the lukewarm breakfast.

Rogan left her alone. He'd apparently picked up on the fact that she really, really did not want to talk.

Finally, she pushed the tray away and pulled the covers up and closed her eyes.

When she woke the next time, it was eleven in the morning. Rogan sat in the visitor chair fiddling with an iPhone. Michael wasn't in his bed.

"The baby…?"

He poked at the phone and slid it into a pocket. "They took him out to weigh him and…I don't know. Whatever things they do."

"My doctor? Has she been here?"

"Not yet. But your mom and dad are here...."

Right then, her mom poked her head around the door. "*M'hija*..."

Elena felt relief. She wouldn't have to be alone with Rogan right now, after all. They wouldn't have to talk. Not yet. She stretched out a hand to her mom.

Luz came in, Javier behind her.

Her mom and dad had brought the car seat for the baby, since Elena was hoping that she and Michael might be released that day. The grandparents stayed for an hour, during which lunch was served and the nurse brought Michael back and said Dr. Sankay wouldn't be in until later in the afternoon.

Before her parents left, her mom bent close, "Are you managing all right, *m'hija*? You and Rogan? Would you like me to stay?"

Yes. Please. Don't leave me alone with him. There's too much to say and I don't know how to say it.

But then she glanced over and saw Rogan watching. And she couldn't do that to him. He clearly wanted to be here, to help with his son. And he had a right to be here.

"No need, *Mami*. Thank you for asking, but we're doing fine."

So her mom kissed her and left.

And then Mercy came. And she bent close, just as Luz had. She asked the same questions, if she was comfortable with only Rogan there. Again, Elena said that she and Rogan were managing great.

After Mercy, Caleb and Irina arrived. They only stayed long enough to congratulate her and admire the baby.

Finally, Davis appeared carrying a huge blue teddy bear. The thing was at least four feet tall. Since most of the available surfaces in the room were already filled with congratulatory flower arrangements, he handed the bear to Rogan, kissed Elena and held Michael. He didn't seem the least surprised to see Rogan there. Apparently, someone in the family had already told him that Rogan was the long-lost father of his new grandson.

When Davis left, it was a little after two. Surely Dr. Sankay would be there any minute now.

But then Rogan set the blue bear on a chair and went over and closed the door all the way. He turned and looked at her. She could see it in his eyes. The big talk was coming. "Elena…"

"You know, I'm really tired." She glanced at the baby in the bassinet at her side. "And he's sleeping. I think I'll just grab a nap, until the doctor comes."

For a moment, she was sure he would insist. But he didn't. He only came to stand over the bed and smooth the blankets that covered her. "Good idea. You need your rest."

She turned over, pulled the sheet up to her chin, shut her eyes and didn't open them again until Dr. Sankay came at quarter of five.

The doctor examined both Elena and the baby and said they were doing very well. Still, she wanted Elena to stay in the hospital until at least the next morning.

"I don't want to keep you here forever," the doctor said. "But I think it's best if new moms and babies stay with us for at least twenty-four hours after the birth."

So it was decided. She was staying the night.

And Rogan was, too, apparently.

After the doctor left, there was dinner. And once the ward clerks had collected the trays, Rogan got his jacket. "I need to do a little shopping—socks and underwear, clean shirts. I'll be back in a couple of hours."

It seemed the perfect opportunity to tell him he really didn't need to stay. "Rogan…"

He paused with the jacket hanging off one arm. "Yeah?"

"You know, it's wonderful that you rushed right down here when Caleb called you. But really, I'm doing fine and so is Michael. And if you need to head back to Dallas, I totally understand. You've been so great, but I know you have your own life and you need to—"

He cut her off. "Trying to get rid of me?" He said it lightly, but there were shadows in his eyes.

And of course, that was exactly what she was trying to do. "It's only, well, I just don't want you to feel that you have to hang around."

He put the jacket on the rest of the way. "But I do have to hang around."

"No, really. You don't."

And then he said the words she'd been dreading. "I don't think we can put it off any longer. We need to talk."

"Well. Um. I know that we do eventually, but—"

He cut her off again. "No. Seriously. I think we need to talk now." He spoke with a hint of bitterness that time. "I think we need to start with why it was Caleb who called me and not you."

She tried not to cringe—and suddenly felt driven to make excuses for herself. "I was going to tell you. I swear it."

"Oh?" He didn't look convinced.

"I was just waiting for Michael to be born." She started explaining—and couldn't seem to stop. "I wanted you to have as much time as possible to yourself, to be free, without having to deal with having a child. And I, well, if you're wondering how I got pregnant with all the protection we used…" Really. She needed to shut up. He was watching her with one eyebrow lifted, not saying a thing. And somehow, she just couldn't stop talking. "I, well, okay. It was like this. I missed one pill the morning after that day my dad had his surgery. But I thought, if we used condoms, it would be safe. It really should have been safe. And I...." She let out a little moan. "I'm sorry, okay? I'm really, really sorry that it turned out like this."

A silence. He was just standing there, watching her. As she met his gaze, he shook his head.

And then he shrugged out of the jacket he'd just put on and tossed it over the chair by the door. He approached her bed.

She looked over at her sleeping baby, longed to pick him up and hold him close. For *her* comfort, not his.

But then Rogan sat beside her on the bed. "It's all right," he said. His voice was gentle. "I don't blame you." Did she believe him? Not completely. His expression was closed to her. If anything, he looked...determined. "We need to move on," he said. "We need to make a life for Michael."

She felt vaguely insulted. Did he think she didn't know that? "I have every intention of making a life for Michael. And of course, I know you'll want time with him. Right now, he needs to be with me, with his mother. You understand that, don't you?" She didn't really want to hear his answer. What if he started talking a custody battle? She forged ahead without waiting for him to reply. "But as soon as he's old enough for solid food, we can start thinking about—"

He put up a hand. "You know me well enough to know that's not going to work for me. I take care of my own and I don't shirk my responsibilities. I want us to get married. I think it's the best way."

Married. God. Just like that? "Rogan, we haven't seen each other for the better part of a year. We spent a week together. A beautiful week, but still. It's not enough to build a marriage on."

He stiffened, drawing those broad shoulders up and back. "Given that we now have Michael, it's going to have to be enough—to start with, anyway. We were…good together. At least, I thought so."

"I thought so, too, but—"

"It will all work out. You'll see."

The thing was, she wanted to say yes. She truly did.

She wanted to just get married, as he said, to try and be a family, and hope that it would all work out.

But what if it didn't?

Wouldn't the conflict and upheaval of a divorce be worse than not getting married in the first place?

"Rogan." She spoke softly. With care. "You…never even called me, you know? Until you found out about the baby yesterday, you were perfectly happy, up in Dallas. Being free."

"Don't characterize me. Please. You have no idea if I've been happy or not." He forked his fingers back over his hair. "And I'm not the only one who didn't call."

"You're right. You're not. But I was the one who made a promise that I would let you go. Those were the terms we set. I was…bound by them. You, well, you didn't make any promises. If you'd wanted to be with me, you could have let me know."

"Look. It doesn't matter who called, or who didn't call."

"It *does* matter. To me, it does."

"Everything's changed now. We have Michael to think about."

"And I *am* thinking of Michael."

He grunted. It was not a happy sound. "If you were thinking of Michael, you would have already said yes. If you were thinking of Michael, you would have called me the minute you found out you were pregnant."

"So then." She held his gaze now. "You *are* angry with me, for not telling you right away."

He looked away, spoke tightly. "That's not the issue."

"Yes. It is. It's very much the issue. All this talk about marriage. We're getting way ahead of ourselves."

"Ahead of ourselves? What is that supposed to mean?"

"It means that we have other things to work through first. We have to…clear the air between us. It's just too soon to consider getting married."

"Too late, if you ask me." He grumbled the words.

She bit back a sharp response and reminded herself that he had been terrific about all of this, rushing to her side the moment he heard about the baby, and sticking with her, *being there* for her and for Michael when it mattered so much.

She couldn't really blame him if he'd finally showed a little of his frustration with the situation. She *didn't* blame him.

Hesitantly, she reached for his hand.

He gave it, which she told herself was a good sign.

She said, "We need time. I'm…not saying no, okay? I'm just saying I need some time to think about it."

"How long?"

"Rogan, come on. Please don't push me."

He pulled his hand free of hers. "I want you to marry me. Right away. I want you and Michael to come back to Dallas with me. The least you can do is to tell me when you'll be willing to give me an answer."

Michael chose that moment to start fussing. He waved his little fists and let out a yelp. She reached over into the bassinet, lifted him out and gathered him to her.

Rogan got up. "I'm going to pick up the things I need.

He needs your full attention now. We can finish this conversation later." He made it sound much more like a threat than a promise.

She put the baby to her shoulder—where he wailed in her ear. "Rogan, I—"

"Later." He turned, grabbed his jacket and walked out the door.

She wanted to call after him, to order him to get back here and finish this important discussion.

But Michael was still crying. And if she started shouting, it would only upset him all the more—not to mention bring the nurses running. "Shh…" She opened her nightgown. He rooted at her breast, still fussing. "Shh. It's okay, okay…"

But she knew that it wasn't.

Rogan's cell rang as he stood at the cash register in the men's department at Dillard's, paying for the underwear, shirts, casual jacket and trousers he'd bought.

As the clerk bagged his purchases, he checked the display and took the call. "Hello, Caleb."

"We need to talk."

He'd known this was coming. "I'm ready."

"You at the hospital?"

"Uh-uh. North Star Mall, picking up a few things I need, since I left Dallas without a suitcase."

"Elena and the baby…?"

"Relax. They're both doing great. The doctor says she's releasing them tomorrow morning."

"Elena expecting you back right away?"

"No," he said flatly. She'd probably be fine with it if he never came back. Too bad. He *would* be back. And one way or another, he would get her agreement that they needed to do the right thing. "You home? I'll come there."

"Good. I'll be waiting."

It was four and a half miles to Caleb's house from the mall. Rogan got there in eight minutes. Caleb was sitting on the front step when he pulled up to the curb.

He rose as Rogan came up the walk. "That was quick."

"Let's get this over with." They went inside. "Where's Irina?"

"She and Hanna are out at Mary and Gabe's place." Gabe was second-born of Caleb's six brothers. Mary and Irina were close friends. "She won't be back for another hour or two."

"Great," Rogan said drily.

"Drink?"

"Might as well."

They went into the living room. Caleb headed for the wet bar and poured them each a scotch on the rocks. He handed Rogan one. And raised the other. "To fatherhood."

Rogan touched his glass to Caleb's and drank. It was good scotch. Smoky and warm going down. "If you're going to punch my lights out, let me put down this cut crystal glass first."

Caleb gestured toward the sofa and a grouping of wing chairs. "Have a seat."

They sat. They sipped.

Finally, Caleb said, "Elena took a leave from her teaching job, did you know? She didn't go back last fall."

"She didn't mention it."

"She's been working for Gabe, secretarial stuff. And also legal research." Gabe Bravo was BravoCorp's attorney. In the family, they called him the fixer. They sent him in whenever there was a problem with a deal they wanted to make. "She's thinking maybe the teaching thing wasn't for her, after all. She's been talking about going back to school, getting a law degree."

"What about the baby?"

"We're all here for her." Caleb put a faint emphasis on the "we're." Meaning Rogan wasn't? "If she wants a law degree, the family—both sides, Bravo and Cabrera—will move heaven and earth to see that she gets whatever she needs to do that."

Meaning that he, Rogan, wouldn't? If she wanted to go to law school, he would support her in that. They could work it out. If she'd only agree to do the right thing and marry him.

Rogan said flatly, "As I already told you, no, she didn't mention any of that."

Caleb looked into his glass, as if there was something endlessly fascinating about ice cubes and scotch. "You got on a plane and got down here fast, as soon as you found out. You've stuck by her side. I guess I'm not going to have to beat the crap out of you, after all."

"Is this where I say how relieved I am?"

"So what now?"

Defensiveness tightened his gut. "What do you mean, what now?"

Caleb sipped his drink. "You know what I mean."

Rogan shrugged. "I've asked her to marry me."

"I was hoping you'd say that—when?"

"An hour ago. She said she needed time to think about it."

"Time? Why?"

"It's what she said, that's all."

"How long did she say she needs?"

"I asked her that same question. She wouldn't answer it. She told me not to push her."

Caleb put his glass down. "You blew it, didn't you?"

Rogan realized he hated this conversation and he really would have preferred if Caleb had just gone ahead and punched his lights out and left the Q&A for some other day.

Caleb prodded, "Didn't you?"

Denials were fruitless. He knew that. "Okay. I'm pretty ticked off at her for not calling me months ago." *And for not mentioning that pill she forgot to take.* And even, now that he was thinking about it, for letting him go, way back in May when he'd made it more than clear that he still wanted to keep seeing her, when they both knew that she wanted to keep seeing him. "And wait a minute. Why didn't *you* call me months ago?"

"You think I didn't want to? Elena refused to speak to me for two months because I kept pushing her to at least let me tell you that she was having a baby. And until I took her to the hospital to have your son, she would never admit that you were the dad. I love my sister, okay? Next to Irina, she's the best friend I've got. I hate it when she's mad at me—now, tell me. *How* did you blow it?"

"So shoot me," Rogan muttered. "I guess I let my anger show."

Caleb was sitting way too still in his chair. "So what you're saying is you really *don't* want to marry her."

"Of course I want to marry her. She's got my kid."

Caleb picked up his glass again—and then set it back down. "You did tell her you love her, right?"

Rogan said nothing. Instead, he cleared his throat and glanced away.

"You didn't tell her you love her." Caleb spoke flatly.

"All right, look. You nailed it. I blew it. Got that? I blew it and I know that I blew it."

"And now you need to make it right."

"You've got all the answers, huh?"

"I've got the answer that matters."

"And do you plan to let me in on the big secret?" Rogan

laid on the sarcasm. But he was sitting forward in his chair. "I mean, if there really is a secret."

"I wouldn't call it a secret. But I know my baby sister. Which means I know what you need to do to get a yes out of her and to get it quick."

"So all right. Lay it on me."

Now Caleb was sitting forward, too. "Listen up and listen good. I'm going to tell you exactly how to get her to say yes—and I'm only going to say it once. I want you clear on what you need to do and I want you out of here before Irina gets home. I don't want her to know that we talked tonight. She's too likely to mention it to Elena and I don't want my sister mad at me. And believe me, she's not going to like it if she knows I told you what to say."

"Women." Rogan shook his head in weariness and wonder.

"Exactly. They want us to say what they want to hear. But they need to believe we made it up all by ourselves."

Chapter Twelve

Elena opened her eyes.

Very strange. There appeared to be several big red hearts floating at the foot of her bed.

Really, she must be dreaming. She shut her eyes again.

And then opened them wide.

The hearts were still there, floating in the air. Shiny hearts…

Wait a minute.

Balloons. Those were heart-shaped Mylar balloons. Big ones. Someone had tied a bunch of balloons to the rail at the foot of the bed.

Who in the world would have…?

She dragged herself up to a sitting position.

And as she did, she noticed there was a new bouquet on the little table beside the bed. A huge one, in a stunning hand-blown vase that swirled with ribbons of color: vivid blue and yellow and coral red. The vase was crowded to overflowing with all kinds of exotic tropical flowers. Freesias. Birds-of-paradise. Anthurium. Tuberoses. Orchids. Lilies. Gardenias. The scent of them drifted in the air the way the shiny red hearts floated at the foot of her bed.

She leaned toward them, breathed them in, closing her eyes again, imagining herself in some secret tropical garden wet with morning dew.

"That first day I saw you—remember?" It was Rogan's voice. Surprised, she glanced toward the sound. He was sitting in the shadowed chair in the far corner of the room. "It was at your dad's office."

She'd been so worried. About him, about the argument they'd had. About everything, really.

But just now he sounded tender. Not angry with her at all. And this moment—so quiet, scented with tuberoses, brightened with shiny hearts—seemed magical.

She felt a sleepy, happy smile curve her lips. "I remember." Her voice came out soft. Slightly husky.

"You took my breath away."

"Oh, Rogan…" So strange. They had fought. He had left. He hadn't returned for hours.

She must have drifted off to sleep.

And now, here he was. With a dozen red balloons. And a gorgeous vase of expensive, sweet-smelling flowers. So different. So…affectionate. So warm.

He spoke in that low, intimate voice again. "You smelled like gardenias. And orange blossoms. And we went out to lunch with your dad and I couldn't stop staring at you. I know I told you this, during that unforgettable week we shared. But I don't think it can hurt to say it again. I wanted you. From that first moment I saw you." He got up then and he came toward her. He wore a new shirt and fresh trousers.

He was so tall and proud, wide-shouldered and strong.

Not handsome, exactly. No. And yet, truly, the best-looking guy she'd ever seen.

He stopped beside the bed and gazed down at her with a hint of a smile curving his mouth.

Her mouth felt dry. "Uh. Water?"

He poured her a cup from the plastic pitcher on the swing-away table and gave it to her, his fingers brushing hers as the cup changed hands.

"Thank you." She sipped, swallowed. Sipped again. And then she gave him the cup back. He set it aside and sat beside her on the edge of the bed. Gently, she chided, "You were...gone a long time."

He reached out, brushed the back of his hand along her cheek. The light touch left sparks of heat in its wake. "I was thinking. About you. About me. And about Michael, too."

She glanced toward the bassinet. "He's so sweet. Especially when he's sleeping."

"Elena."

She felt suddenly shy and couldn't quite make herself look at him. "I'm so sorry, that we...argued earlier."

He touched her chin, guided her face around so that she met his eyes again—green fire, those eyes. "I should have called you, after we separated in May. I *wanted* to call you. But I didn't know...how to begin."

She understood completely. "Yes. It was the same for me. A hundred times—a *thousand* times—I picked up the phone to call you. I always chickened out at that last possible second."

"Me, too." He caught her fingers, pressed his warm, soft lips to the back of her hand.

She trembled at the caress, at the feel of his breath against her skin. "I do want us to...work it out."

"I love you, Elena."

Just like that, so simply, he had said the words. The words that meant so much.

The words that meant everything to her.

She could hardly believe she had actually heard them. "Rogan. You're, um, serious?"

He pressed her hand to the crisp front of his new shirt, slipping his thumb beneath her fingers, guiding them to open, so she could feel his warm, solid chest. And the steady, strong beating of his heart.

She kept picturing him tiptoeing around the dim hospital room, trying not to wake her as he tied the balloons to the bed and set the beautiful flower arrangement just so on the bedside table, where she would see it when she woke up.

He held her gaze so intently. And he said those magic words again. "I love you. I want you. Always. That will never change. And I'm glad for Michael, that we have Michael. But I'm here for *you*, too. For you, first and foremost."

Her throat clutched. She swallowed to loosen it. Could he have said it more perfectly? It didn't seem possible that he could have.

How could he have known just the right words to say?

This man loves me. He wants to make a life with me....

Within her, something went soft and pliant. A carefully erected barrier dissolved. She felt herself open to him.

Like a flower spreading its petals to welcome the sun.

He said it again. "I love you. I want to be with you. I want our family. That's how it should be. You, me and Michael. Together."

She could hold back no longer. "I...I love you, too, Rogan." There. She had said it. She had confessed the truth. To herself, as much as to him. "I love you so much."

He raised his free hand, turned it over, opened it.

She gasped at what waited, glittering, in the heart of his palm: a diamond ring and matching wedding band.

So beautiful. So perfect. A set she might have chosen for herself. Vintage style, with a pure, large central stone, two slightly smaller diamonds flanking it and pavé diamonds cut into the bands of both the wedding band and the engagement ring.

She tried to find words. "Wh…where did you find them?"

He named a jeweler. "They were open. I went in. I saw this engagement ring and decided it was the one."

"Tonight? You did this tonight?"

His smile was wry and tender. "It was the first chance I've had."

"And the flowers. The balloons. It's like a dream, you know?"

"Let me say this again, okay?"

"Oh, Rogan…"

"Marry me, Elena. I love you more than words can possibly say. Marry me and make me the happiest man alive."

She wanted to say yes, right then. To grab that ring and put it on and never, ever let it off her finger for as long as she lived.

And yet…

"Rogan, there are so many things we probably should talk about."

A frown creased his brow—and then quickly vanished. "You're right, of course. And we will. We'll work together, to make a life that's good for both of us. I've been thinking…"

"Uh, you have?"

"Oh, yeah. Maybe you don't want to live in Dallas. I can understand that. With your family, everyone you care about here, in San Antonio, this might be a better place for us."

"You would do that?" She asked the question prayerfully. "You would move here?"

He nodded. "I can move my headquarters here, to the branch I bought from your dad. It *would* take time, though."

She dared to reach out, to touch the side of his face. Smooth. He must have shaved, too. All this preparation, to make everything just right. For her. For this moment, when he asked her again to be his wife. Asked her in such a way that she could hardly remember why she'd said no the first time.

"I would be willing to be patient," she said.

"You would?" He looked so hopeful.

She nodded, eagerly. "And, well, Dallas isn't *that* far away. I'm the most able to move now. So I would move there, with you. And then we could take our time, think it over, plan out the long-term goals."

"It's all workable. You're so right."

She had so many things she wanted to tell him now. A thousand things. "I haven't really had a chance to tell you, but I quit my teaching job. I've been working for Gabe—you remember Gabe, the family lawyer? Gabe's a great boss. And I've found I'm interested in the law. And eventually, when Michael's a little older, I want to go to law school. I was thinking Austin. But I could go to St. Mary's here. Or even Texas Wesleyan in Fort Worth. There are lots of options—I mean, as long as we were both flexible. As long as we were communicating, working together, you know?"

"I do, Elena. I know." He drew her hand to his lips again, kissed it so tenderly. "Marry me."

All her doubts seem to have melted away. He loved her. She loved him.

What else was there to say? "Yes. I will, Rogan. I would be proud to be your wife."

Chapter Thirteen

In Texas, there was a seventy-two hour waiting period before a couple could marry after acquiring a license.

They got the license Monday when the courthouse opened.

And they married Thursday afternoon. Yes, they were both Catholics and would have preferred a wedding in the church. But that would take months. They would have to sign up for a date well in advance and go through counseling beforehand.

They didn't want to wait. They were both anxious to begin their lives together, as a family. Their marriage, they agreed, was forever. Whether they shared their vows before a priest on consecrated ground.

Or not.

The minister from Davis and Aleta's church agreed to officiate. And they said their vows in the front living room at Bravo Ridge. It was raining that day, the sky a leaden gray. The wind was wild outside. The rain made splattering sounds as it beat against the room's distinctive high, arched windows. It ran down the panes in tiny jeweled rivers.

To Elena, the day was like a dream.

Everyone was smiling and kind, so happy for her and Rogan. She wore a new dress she'd bought the day before, tea length, chiffon and lace, with cap sleeves and a scoop neck. She had a short veil, too, and lacy wrist-length white gloves. She carried a bouquet of gardenias and freesias.

Her dad walked her down the makeshift aisle between five rows of chairs set up for the ceremony. So many family members had managed to get away for the day to be there. That pleased her so much. She felt so happy and a little bit stunned—and she tried not to worry that her milk might leak and stain her pretty new dress.

It all seemed to be happening so fast. Tomorrow, she and Rogan would fly to Dallas. She would start a whole new life.

But it was right, she knew it.

She and Rogan had agreed that they wanted their baby to be with them as they said their vows. And now, as she walked slowly toward him, Rogan waited by the minister, wearing a beautiful chalk stripe blue suit, holding Michael in his arms. She looked at her groom and only at him as she slowly went to meet him.

Javier stepped aside. She gave her bouquet to Mercy, her one attendant. And she held out her hands for the bundle in blue.

Rogan gave Michael to her. She gathered her son close and glanced down at his sleeping face. He looked so peaceful, so content at that moment. As if he knew that all was right in his world.

The minister began to speak. "We are gathered here together…"

* * *

After the ceremony, there was champagne. Luz took the baby and Elena accepted a glass and even dared to treat herself to a couple of sips. It seemed everyone had a toast to offer.

Before the big dinner in the formal dining room, Caleb pulled her aside, into one of the unoccupied rooms along the hallway between the kitchen and the game room. "I just need to know that you're happy, that's all."

She hugged him. "I am. So happy." She stood back, turned in a circle. "Can't you tell?"

He took her by the shoulders and gazed at her, a funny half smile curving his lips. "You make a gorgeous bride, you know that?"

She thought he looked a little…sheepish, maybe. "Thank you. And have you done something you shouldn't have?"

He chuckled. That slightly guilty look was gone. Maybe she'd only imagined it. "Me? Never. As soon as you're settled in, we're coming to visit."

"I can't wait."

"I mean it. Be happy."

"I promise I will."

Elena hugged him again and then had to hurry off to feed Michael before they all sat down to eat.

After the meal, there was more champagne. And a little later, Elena and Rogan cut the cake. Elena's half sister Zoe was a really talented amateur photographer. She let her husband, Dax, take care of their nine-month-old, Zachary, and took a lot of pictures that day. Zoe must have snapped twenty or thirty just of them cutting that pretty white three-tiered cake, with Rogan slightly behind Elena, his hand over hers on the sterling silver knife. They laughed as they fed each other pieces much too big to fit into their mouths.

And then he kissed her. "Sweetest kiss I ever had," he said.

And he was right, too. She had cake and frosting smeared all over her face.

She threw the bouquet from the spiral staircase in the foyer. Brenda, Rogan's sister, caught it. A good thing, too, given that she was the only single woman there.

Brenda had blue eyes and light brown hair cut short and spiky. The cute, funky style suited her personality. She'd flown in from New York City the night before to be there for her brother's wedding, and she was going back tomorrow morning in order not to miss school. Cormac and Niall had made it, too. Elena was pleased they'd been able to come— and grateful to Davis, who'd insisted they all three would stay at the ranch.

By nine that evening, Elena was starting to droop a little. It was a week since she'd delivered Michael and she still tired easily. Plus, her nights were no longer her own. She was up and down constantly, for feedings and diaper changes. Rogan was a sweetheart and helped her out as much as he could. Still, she slept in fits and starts, waking whenever her baby cried.

She was in the living room, holding Michael, chatting with Brenda when Rogan's strong arms came around her. "I'm thinking it's about time I carried you out of here." He brushed a kiss against her temple.

She leaned back into his embrace with a sigh. "Good idea. Before I fall over from total exhaustion."

Brenda set down her champagne glass. "Let me hold my nephew. You guys can go and tell them all goodbye."

Everyone piled out onto the front veranda to watch them drive away, trailing the ridiculous tin cans someone had snuck out and tied to the bumper. She waved and they all waved back, laughing, calling out random bits of silly advice.

"Don't do anything we wouldn't do—or if you do, take pictures!"

"Rogan, keep your hands on the wheel and your eyes on the road!"

"Elena, go to bed when you get home—and to sleep!"

She chuckled at that one. They weren't doing much but sleeping when they went to bed. It would be weeks before they could have a real wedding night.

If Michael ever gave them an hour or two to themselves.

Cans clanging, they rolled around the circular drive and headed off toward the highway. Destination: her condo, where they were spending their last night in San Antonio.

When they got there, he made her stand out on the landing while he carried Michael in and put him in his bassinet. He was back in no time, sweeping her up into his strong arms, carrying her over the threshold.

She laughed, "Are you going to do this again, when we get to your house in Dallas?"

"*Our* house," he corrected. "And the answer is yes."

And then he kissed her, a beautiful, long deep kiss—a kiss that almost made up for the wedding night they weren't going to have.

"Mrs. Murdoch," he whispered, sounding very satisfied with the sound of that, as he slowly let her feet slide back to the floor in the middle of all of their luggage, packed and ready for the trip tomorrow. Eventually, she would come back down to SA, pack up the rest of her things and put the condo on the market. "Elena Murdoch. I like the sound of that."

They stood in the open doorway, hardly caring that the night air was brisk and chilly after the rain.

"I like it, too," she told him.

"We are going to be so happy," he said.

She agreed, "Oh, yes we are." She reached over and shoved the door shut.

He kissed her again as he scooped her high once more and carried her down the hall.

And for the most part, in the weeks that followed, they *were* happy.

The day after the wedding, they drove to Dallas in her car. On the way up through the Hill Country, he told her that if she didn't like the house, they could choose another one together. Or he would build them one.

Laughing, she leaned across the console for a quick kiss. "How about if I get a look at it first before you start worrying I'm not going to like it?"

She loved the house on sight. It was a two-story four-bedroom in Highland Park, an upscale Dallas neighborhood. Instead of building it himself, he'd remodeled a traditional two-story house built in 1938. The kitchen was roomy and modern and there were big windows everywhere, with beautiful views of the multileveled backyard and the wide sweep of lawn in front.

When he carried her over the threshold, he said, "Welcome home, Mrs. Murdoch." And he kissed her.

She looked in his eyes and knew she was exactly where she was meant to be. She whispered, "I love you, Rogan."

And he kissed her again as he eased her back down onto her own two feet.

That was the moment, she thought later. The exact moment when she began to suspect that all was not as she imagined it to be.

It was the first time she noticed that he hadn't said he loved her, too.

No, it wasn't a big deal. He was good to her, very much there for her, there *with* her when they were together. He was truly *loving* to her. And that was what mattered.

But was there some significance to his not actually saying the words?

When she looked back, she couldn't remember him saying those words since the night he proposed.

He hadn't said them on their wedding day, except during the vows, when he promised to love, honor and cherish her. He hadn't said them at any time in the hectic, exhausting three days before their wedding day, either. She was sure of it.

He hadn't said "I love you" once since that magical night in the hospital, when they'd argued and he'd walked out on her because she wouldn't agree to marry him—and then reappeared hours later with balloon hearts and the most beautiful bouquet of flowers she'd ever seen.

Reappeared a changed man. One who said all the right things, all the most romantic, beautiful things. A man who eased all her fears about the idea of a life with him, about whether it was really the right choice for them. A man who declared his love openly, beautifully—and frequently.

Looking back, she realized he must have said he loved her ten times that wonderful night.

And not once since. Was that a little strange? It seemed strange to her.

She thought about just asking him, *By the way, Rogan. Do you love me?*

Or maybe…

Ahem. Rogan. I've noticed you haven't said you love me since the night you proposed.

But that seemed…a little pushy, didn't it? A little bit needy. Was she that insecure, that she had to ask her husband if he loved her?

As one day became the next and she was busy with Michael and with building a new life in a new town, she did wonder. If there might be something going on with him that she didn't get, didn't understand. She wondered if it maybe had to do with his freedom issues—and yes. That was how she was coming to think of them.

As his freedom issues.

He seemed happy. He really did. But sometimes she just had the feeling that he still clung to that longing, deep down. That he still yearned for the single life he'd enjoyed so briefly.

That maybe he felt cheated. Just a little.

She joined a breast-feeding group and quickly made new friends. They had Cormac over often. Sometimes he brought a date. Sometimes he just showed up alone. But she enjoyed hanging around with him and she was happy to have extended family right there in town. She also got to know Victor Lukovic, whom Irina Bravo considered a brother, and who had gone to UT with Rogan and Caleb.

Elena and Maddy Liz, Victor's wife, became good friends right away. Maddy was a Dallas deb, born and bred. She was gorgeous, smart and fun to be around. She knew everyone. And she was only too eager to introduce Elena to all her Junior League friends.

Life was good. Life was excellent.

She kept telling herself that she was just being paranoid, to worry simply because her husband didn't say those three little words. He was affectionate with her and he came home for dinner every night. He adored his son. No, they hadn't made love yet. She didn't have her new doctor's go-ahead on that.

But sometimes, in the evening after dinner, while Michael was napping, they would start to watch a movie—and end up all over each other. She had no doubt that he wanted her, maybe as much as she wanted him.

It was on one of those nights, after they'd been making out on the sofa until their lips almost fell off, that she whispered, "I love you."

And he did what he always did when she said that— nothing. Except to pull her close and kiss her some more.

Eventually, Michael started fussing and she went to get him. She sat in the rocker in the family room to nurse him. Rogan turned off the movie. They'd been smooching through so much of it, neither of them had followed what was happening on the screen anyway.

He tossed the remote onto the coffee table. "Think I'll get a beer. You want something?"

She shook her head—and the words just kind of rose to her lips and spilled on out. "Do you love me, Rogan?"

He said what she'd known he would say. "Of course I do."

And she went even further with it. "You know, when I tell you I love you, you never say it back to me."

He frowned. And then he got up and came over to the rocker. He bent down and he kissed her, a lovely, light kiss. "I love you, Elena."

And she smiled against his lips. "Good. I love you, too."

She should have been satisfied with that. She told herself she *was* satisfied. Absolutely.

A few days later, Brenda came home from New York City to spend four days with them during her spring break. She was as bright and fun as Elena remembered. They went shopping together and Niall came up from Austin on Brenda's third day home. They had a family dinner on Friday night, all the Murdoch siblings together, along with Victor and Maddy Liz and their three kids. Elena took a bunch of pictures. It was a great dinner party to cap off a wonderful visit.

Brenda was set to fly back to Manhattan Saturday afternoon. That morning, Rogan made his famous French toast for breakfast. Niall left at eleven. After that, they hung around the house, enjoying the last hours of Brenda's visit before they took her to the airport at two o'clock.

Around one-thirty, when Brenda was up in her room getting all her stuff together to go, Elena found the battered script for the play Rogan's sister was rehearsing abandoned on the laundry room folding table. She grabbed it and headed for the stairs.

At the landing on the second floor, she saw that Brenda's door was open. As she approached, she could hear Brenda in there talking on the phone.

"She's great. I love her. And you should see my new nephew. Uh, yeah. Adorable…" A silence. And when Brenda spoke again, she lowered the volume to a more confidential level. "I know, I know. Big shocker. Rogan always swore he wouldn't get married until he was old and gray—not after raising the three of us. Niall especially. Well, you remember. Nightmare. But hey, well, Elena is amazing and there *is* my darling nephew to think about…. What?… Yeah. Of course he would marry her. That's who he is. And it's not like he's going to suffer all that much because his life didn't turn out as planned. She's not only a good person and fun to hang with, she's really hot-looking. And she can cook."

Elena stood, frozen, a foot or two from that open door. Her face felt like someone had struck a match to it. Burning with shame.

It wasn't anything bad Brenda had said, exactly. It wasn't anything Elena didn't already know.

It was just…

Of course he would marry her. That's who he is.

And it's not like he's going to suffer all that much because his life didn't turn out as planned.

Beyond the open door, Brenda was still talking—at full volume, again. "I know. I'm sorry. Completely my bad and I will make it up to you. Next time, I promise…" And then she was on to how much she loved her life in New York.

Slowly, still clutching the tattered script in her hand, Elena turned and retraced her steps. Down the stairs, through the living room and the family room, into the laundry room off the kitchen.

She shut the door and leaned her forehead against it and wondered why she felt so terrible about this.

Really, she kept telling herself, it just wasn't anything that awful. It only *felt* awful.

As if she'd somehow been tricked into believing that Rogan was someone he wasn't.

She found herself thinking about that night in the hospital, the night he proposed, about the night and day difference between the angry, determined man who had walked out on her at six—and the tender, romantic dream guy who had returned at eleven spouting words of love. Really, she needed to sit down with him and talk about this. She was letting her doubts about his true feelings get in the way of her love for him.

Tonight, she promised herself. *Tonight, when we're alone, we'll have a long talk about this….*

But then, well, the rest of the day passed. And she started thinking that she had overreacted.

They took Brenda to the airport. Brenda grabbed Elena in a goodbye hug and whispered, "I am so glad to have you for my sister-in-law. I cannot tell you. Just really, really glad." She said it with feeling and when she pulled back, she had tears in her eyes. She said, "My big brother is a very lucky man."

They went home, had dinner, made out like a couple of kids on the family room couch.

And she decided she had taken the things she'd overheard Brenda saying way too seriously. She needed to forget all these vague doubts and enjoy the great life she and Rogan shared.

Monday, she saw her new OB-GYN. And she got the go-ahead to do more than smooch on the couch. It was only five weeks and two days since she'd had Michael, but her doctor assured her that it would be safe.

On her way home, she stopped and bought a hundred dollar bottle of champagne. And for dinner, she slathered a prime rib with her own special dill and garlic rub. She baked a couple of giant Idaho potatoes and did the green beans with almonds, just the way her husband liked them best.

And when Rogan got home from work, she met him at the front door wearing lingerie she'd bought shopping with Brenda, a wisp of peach silk that showed a whole lot more than it covered. They made love right there in the foyer, standing up.

By the time he slowly let her feet slide down to touch the floor again, she had no doubt that her husband still thought she was sexy and desirable.

Later, after she fed Michael and Rogan did diaper duty, they shared a champagne toast, ate their prime rib dinner— and went to bed to celebrate some more.

No, he never once said he loved her, though she said it several times that night.

But it didn't matter, she told herself. He *showed* that he loved her in so many ways. Life was good. Life was amazing.

They had it all.

And then, on Friday, Caleb and Irina came up with baby Hanna for the weekend. It was a great visit. Friday night, they all went over to Victor and Maddy Liz's for dinner.

Saturday night, Elena cooked just for the four of them—five, including Hanna, who sat quietly in her high chair with bits of apple and grapes to munch on. Hanna got fussy around eight-thirty, so Irina took her upstairs to get her ready for bed.

And then, just a minute or two after Irina went up, Michael, who had slept through the grown-ups' dinner, started fussing in his crib. Elena went up to nurse him.

He fell asleep quickly. She tucked him into bed again, pressed a kiss on his perfect little cheek and went back down to join the others. As she passed the guestroom, she heard Irina's voice in there, singing a lullaby in Argovian, the language of her childhood.

She almost tapped on the door and went in to sit with her sister-in-law while she sang baby Hanna to sleep.

But no. Disturbing them would only wake Hanna up all over again. So she went on down the stairs. At the bottom, she could hear the low murmur of the men's voices in the dining room.

Something about their hushed tones made her hesitate in the shadowed living room, with her hand on the newel post.

"Don't get all defensive on me." Caleb's voice. "It looks to me like it's working out great, is all I'm saying."

"Just shut up about it." Rogan growled the words. "You said yourself she could never know." *She, who?* "One of them could be back down here any second now."

One of them?

So it was something neither she nor Irina was supposed to know.

This was ridiculous. She thought of the way she'd be-haved a week ago, running downstairs and hiding in the laundry room because she'd happened to overhear Brenda talking about her on the phone.

Uh-uh. Enough. She turned and headed for the dining room.

Caleb was talking again. "Don't worry. They just went up. Come on. Admit it. You're happy being married. I did you a good turn. Sometimes a man just needs a little push to get it right."

Elena reached the dining room door by then. She went on in. "A little push to get *what* right?"

Chapter Fourteen

Caleb almost dropped the glass of brandy he was sipping.

But Rogan didn't so much as blink. "Nothing—he went right back to sleep, huh?"

For a moment, Elena considered getting pushy, demanding to know what in the world they were whispering about, telling them she wasn't backing off until they explained what was going on.

But then again, why ruin the evening? Now was neither the time nor the place.

Later. After their guests had gone back to San Antonio.

She smiled and snapped her fingers. "Out like a light."

A few minutes after that, Irina rejoined them. Elena served the dessert.

More than once that evening, Elena found Caleb watching her. Was he nervous about something?

She had a feeling he was. And she *would* be finding out what.

All in good time.

Caleb and his family left on Sunday morning.

Elena waited until after lunch, when she'd just put Michael in his crib after a feeding, to bring up the issue of what she'd overheard Saturday night. She found Rogan sitting at the computer in his study at the front of the house.

He looked up when she stepped into the open doorway.

She leaned against the doorframe, feeling absurdly weak-kneed all of a sudden. "It's, um, about Saturday night. I've been wondering what you and Caleb were talking about at the table when Irina and I went upstairs...."

"I told you it was nothing." His expression, like his voice, was flat. Careful.

She entered the study, perched on a chair by the door. "Rogan..." She managed his name and then didn't know where to go from there.

And he wasn't helping. "Can we talk about this later? I've got some things to catch up on here."

She wavered, asking herself, was it really so important? Did it really matter that much? He was good to her. If he and Caleb wanted to have a few secrets between themselves, what could that hurt?

He was frowning. "Something else?"

"When *can* we talk about it?"

He picked up the pen on his desk pad, tapped the desk with it. "Seriously. There's nothing to talk about."

Again, she had to hold herself there, in the chair, to keep after him about this when he so clearly did not want to discuss it. Whatever *it* was. "I heard you tell Caleb to be quiet, that Irina or I could come back downstairs any minute. What was it you didn't want me to hear?"

He tossed the pen down. "All right. Fine."

"You look so…angry."

"I'm not angry. Caleb gave me a few…pointers, okay?"

"Pointers about what?"

Rogan sat back in his swivel chair, stretched his big arms behind his head and then sat forward again. "I said it doesn't matter. It doesn't. Can't you just take my word on that and let it be?"

"I only want to understand."

"There's nothing to understand."

What would Caleb not want her to know?

It came to her: that he'd interfered between her and Rogan again.

Was that it?

She said, "That night you proposed to me. In the hospital. We argued. You left. You came back hours later and you were like a different man…."

He braced an elbow on the desk, rubbed the bridge of his nose between his thumb and forefinger. "Let it be, will you?"

She didn't. She couldn't. "You went to Caleb, didn't you?"

He slapped his palm, flat, on the desk top. She winced at the sound. "I did not *go* to Caleb."

"Let me put it this way. Did you see my brother between when you left the hospital that night and when you came back?"

He looked away, toward the window and the bright afternoon outside. "It's not that big of a deal, you know?"

"I think it is. I think it's something that I really need to understand. I think it's the key to what isn't…right between us."

"What do you mean, what isn't right? Everything's fine."

"Yes. That's true. In some ways, it is. But I feel…like you're hiding something from me, Rogan. Something you really need to talk to me about."

"What do you want from me, Elena?"

"Just the truth. That's all. What happened that night?"

He took in a slow breath and let it out hard. "Fine. Caleb called me. I went over there, figuring he was going to pop me a good one for messing with his innocent baby sister. But what he was really interested in was if I was going to marry you. I told him I damn well was. But that you had turned me down."

"And he gave you…pointers?"

"Yeah. That's right. Pointers." Now he was glaring at her. "That's all of it. That's the big freaking secret. He gave me a few pointers and I took them to heart. And it all worked out fine."

"What pointers?"

"Damn it, Elena."

"What pointers?"

He glared some more. She glared right back.

Finally, he said, "Caleb said that you're not really who you like to think you are."

"Excuse me?"

"He said that you consider yourself a realist, independent. Practical. But really, you're a romantic to the core. He said you'd waited your whole life for the right guy and I was it, that you never would have been with me, if I wasn't. He said…" The words ran out. He shook his head. "It's enough."

"Tell me the rest."

"Elena…"

"The rest."

"Fine. All right. He said that if I was serious about marrying you, I had to say that I love you. And I had to make you believe it. I had to convince you that you're the only woman for me. He said I had to be romantic about it—and he said you could never know it wasn't all my idea because a woman needs to think her guy knows what to say without being coached."

She was shaking her head now. "The flowers. The ring. The words you said…"

He nodded. His green eyes were bleak as a winter sea. "Yeah. Caleb gives good advice, huh?"

"I'm going to kill him."

"Which is why he didn't want you ever to know."

"Too bad he just had to gloat about it last night."

"Yeah," Rogan agreed way too quietly. "Completely blows that he did that, I gotta say."

"But he was wrong about one thing."

"Yeah?" He didn't look all that excited to hear what.

She told him anyway. "A woman doesn't care so much if a man needs a few pointers. As long as he's…sincere, you know? As long as when he says he loves her, he really means it."

Rogan winced. And then he braced both elbows on the desk and rubbed his eyes. "Of course I meant it."

"You're sounding a little…automatic. You know that?"

He said nothing. He just sat there.

She got up, then. She went over to the window and stood staring out at the long front walk, at the old live oak in the center of the lawn with its thick, wide branches spreading up to the blue Texas sky. "I think you lied to me, Rogan. You said that you *really* wanted to marry me—for *me*, not just because I had your baby. You said you loved me. And that night, you really seemed to mean it. But you've never said it again after that, not without me prompting you."

"What does it matter?" he said to her back. "We're happy, aren't we? We have a good life together. Why do you have to make a big deal out of this…this love thing? About a few little words and whether I say them without you pushing me, about *how* I say them when I say them. I just don't get it. It makes no sense."

She turned to face him then. "I think you do get it. I think you know exactly what you did."

"What I did? What I did was marry you. Was that so wrong?"

"You lied."

He didn't deny it. She knew why. Because he *had* lied.

She spoke again, schooling her voice to a gentle, even tone. "Oh, Rogan. Caleb got a lot of it right. I *am* a romantic. And I want the man I love to love me in return. I want him to *tell* me he loves me. And I want him to mean it. And you got me to marry you by telling me what I wanted to hear and being really, really convincing about it. You lied, that's what you did. And I just want you to tell me, admit to my face that you lied."

"I didn't lie. I…" The sentence trailed off without ever really getting started.

She refused to back off. "I want to know, okay? I want to know what you were really thinking that night, what was really going through your mind the first time you started in on me about marriage. The time you got angry and walked out."

He shoved back his chair and stood. "There's no point in rehashing all this. This is a bunch of noise about nothing. You have to see that."

She stood very still, facing him, in front of the window.

Funny, how calm she felt given that her heart was breaking. "Are you going to walk out on me again?"

"I didn't say I was walking out."

"You didn't have to say it. I can see it in your eyes."

He looked like he wanted to break something. And he asked, for the second time, "What do you want from me, Elena?"

Her answer remained the same. "I want the truth. That's all. Just the truth."

Rogan said nothing. He didn't trust himself to speak. This was a truly stupid conversation.

So why was he so pissed off at her that he could hardly see straight?

She was waiting, just standing there in front of the sunlit window. Waiting for him to tell her what they both knew she didn't really want to hear.

"This is a bad idea," he warned. Again.

And still, she just stood there, watching him. Waiting.

And he was getting angrier. "Look. You messed me over, okay? And that night in the hospital when I tried to get you to do the right thing and agree to marry me, I was seriously pissed off about that, about the way you messed me over."

She flinched. But she didn't say she'd heard enough. "Go on."

"You don't want to hear this."

"Yes. Yes, I do."

"All right. You asked for it." He dropped back to his chair. "You should have told me, that first night we were together, that night at the very end of April, that you'd screwed up with the birth control pills. I had a right to have all the information you had."

She put a hand against her chest, as if her heart was

doing scary things in there. But still, she held her ground. "Yeah. I get that. I do. I was wrong not to tell you. I…made all kinds of excuses for why I didn't need to tell you. That it was only one pill. That I had the condoms and as long as we used them, we would be safe."

"I might have walked away that first night, if you'd told me."

Her soft mouth trembled. "Oh, God…"

And he made himself confess, "It's doubtful. Because I wanted you. Bad. And we did have the condoms. But still. You took that choice away from me."

"I know. Oh, Rogan. I see that." She sucked in a trembling breath, glanced toward the open door longingly. But then she stiffened, and made herself meet his eyes again. "What else?"

"You didn't call me when you found out you were pregnant. You let months go by. I wouldn't even have been there to see Michael born, if Caleb hadn't taken action. As soon as you got pregnant, I was involved. I had a right to know. But you ignored my rights. You took away my choices. Again."

Her big eyes were shiny with tears now. She swallowed, convulsively. "You're right. I know you're right. I…screwed up. I always planned to tell you. And I *would* have. I swear it. But I told myself you didn't need to know. Not yet. Not until the baby was born."

"I did need to know."

"I…I see that now. I do." She swallowed again, blinked away the tears in her eyes. "What else?"

"It's enough."

"What else?"

He waved a hand. "All right. One last thing. Back in May, before I left, I told you I wanted to keep seeing you. You turned me down."

She was shaking her head. "No." Her chin had a mutinous tilt. "Don't you get on me for that. It was the agreement we had. It was what you wanted. To be free. Don't you dare try and tell me you don't remember that you wanted to be free."

"Of course I remember."

"Well, good then. My not telling you about the pill I missed, not telling you right away that I was pregnant... I was in the wrong on both counts. And I can understand why you're having trouble getting past those things I didn't do. But if you're holding it against me that I gave you what you said you wanted—that I set you free, let you go—well, that's not right. And you know it's not."

"You could have just...let it happen, between us. You were too damn proud, Elena. You had to have it all locked up with us—an expiration date. Or forever."

Her mouth was trembling again. "No. That's not true. All I wanted was a little hope that at some point you might see a future for us. You wouldn't give me that hope. I saw no point in holding on."

"I saw it differently."

"Fine. What else?"

"What else? Isn't that enough for one day?"

She pressed her lips together, tilted her chin high again. "One more thing."

"Sure. Hit me with it."

"Why wouldn't you talk to me *then,* that night in the hospital, about all the ways you're angry with me?"

"Oh, come on. What for? What good would it have done? What good does it do *now,* except to make me feel like a jerk and to make you want to cry?"

"We can't just go around lying to each other. It's not a healthy way to be. My mother lied to my dad for over twenty years. And when the truth finally came out, it almost destroyed both of them. And it wasn't so great for me or my sister, either."

"My having a few resentments toward you is not the same as your mom sleeping with Davis Bravo behind your dad's back."

"No, it's not. But if you asked them how it could possibly have happened that my mother, who loved my dad more than her life, ended up betraying him with his worst enemy, I know they would tell you that it started with resentment and anger between them. *Unresolved* resentment. Anger that they didn't deal with honestly."

"It's not the same," he said again. Maybe this time she would hear him.

But she didn't. "A lie is a lie," she said. "And instead of your lying to me that night in the hospital, instead of your telling me you loved me when you didn't in order to get me to agree to marry you, we should have been talking about the hard things, about the ways you were—and are—so very angry with me."

He really didn't get why she refused to see the light on this. "You'd just had a baby. The last thing you needed was for me to unload all my garbage on you."

"Then we could have waited. Until I'd recovered a little."

"What do you mean, waited? We needed to be married." His voice had way too much heat in it. He tamped the fury down. "Our son needed both of his parents. Waiting would have only given you more time to think of all the reasons we didn't need to be married."

"That's not true."

"I think it is. I did what I had to do to make you my wife, to make a family for Michael."

Her eyes were dry now. And she looked across the distance between them without saying anything for the longest time. Finally, she came out with it. "You only said you loved me because Caleb told you that was the way to get me to marry you."

"Well. It was, wasn't it?"

"Rogan. You tricked me."

"I told you what you needed to hear to make you do the right thing."

"The right thing."

"That's what I said."

"How can such a smart man be so foolish?" She started toward him and she kept coming until she stood beside the desk, looking down at him. When she spoke, her voice was low and deliberate. "There is one thing I feared the most and it's happened. That you would think I stole your chance at freedom from you and you would resent me for it. It was why I said no to you when you asked me to marry you the first time. Why I *should* have said no when you came back with the balloons and the flowers, the perfect ring and the tender words of love. And now, well, here we are. Married. And on the surface, everything has seemed so great. Everything has looked so wonderful. But underneath, Rogan. Underneath, a storm is brewing. Underneath, you hold your resentment close to your heart. And until you're able to let it go, things can never be truly right between us."

Chapter Fifteen

Nothing changed.

They got through each day. Elena still had dinner waiting when Rogan came home at night. They slept together. They both took loving care of Michael.

But everything was different.

They didn't make love. They each kept strictly to their own separate sides of the king-size bed. They spoke gently to each other when they had to—about errands that needed running, about obligations they had agreed to fulfill—gently, not tenderly. They were in the same room often, but they avoided eye contact.

A deep silence had grown between them.

Elena tried to tell herself that the silence was necessary. They had married when they probably shouldn't have— too soon, certainly. But now they *were* married. And she believed in that, in the sanctity of the marriage vows. She knew that he did, too.

There would be no divorce. Even if they never found their way to a true union as man and wife.

The irony of the situation didn't escape her. She and Rogan were starting to remind her of her parents. No, she hadn't slept with her father's enemy. Her baby was not another man's child. But there was a yawning rift in her marriage, a deep wound between herself and her husband.

She wasn't sure how to bridge that rift, how to heal the wound. Sometimes she thought she ought to know what to do. And sometimes she thought that it wasn't her place to take the next shot at the problem. That she'd done more than enough on Sunday in his office.

Way more than enough and not in a good way.

She reminded herself that her parents had worked out their differences in the end, that now Javier and Luz Cabrera had a stronger marriage than before. That should have comforted her. Too bad it only reminded her that it had taken a three-year separation and her dad's heart attack to make them see the light and reunite.

Midweek, Irina called to say how much she and Caleb had enjoyed the weekend. Elena kept the conversation light and pleasant, not revealing the new emptiness in her heart and her life.

She'd decided not to confront Caleb—not for a while, anyway. Not until she could talk to him without yelling at him, without wanting to strangle him.

And then, wouldn't you know? He called her.

"Something's wrong," he said without so much as a hello. "Rogan won't return my calls. What's going on?"

So she told him that she'd pushed Rogan until he confessed that Caleb had coached him on how to propose. "Then we had...words, Caleb. Very hard words. My husband and I aren't getting along all that well right now."

Caleb said, "What can I do? Anything. Whatever you need. I want to help."

She wanted to shout at him to mind his own damn business. She wanted to call him a few very bad names. But she knew that he loved her and she did love him. So she spoke with slow care. "Listen to me, big brother. Do. Not. Help. Are we clear on that?"

A silence. "You're mad at me."

"Yes, I am. Very much so. I'll get over it. Eventually. But before I do, I need your promise that you will never—ever—try to manipulate me again."

"I didn't—"

"Stop. Don't say it. I don't want to hear it. Yes, you did manipulate me—or at least, you told my husband how to manipulate me. That was a rotten thing for you to do."

"I only wanted—"

"No excuses, please. I know you meant well. You always do. But meaning well is not enough. Don't do it again."

"I'm sorry." He sounded sincere. "I screwed up."

"Yeah. You did."

"And okay, you have my word. I will never in any way manipulate you again."

"Not even if you're *sure* it's the best thing you could do for me?" She piled on the sarcasm.

He made a low grumbling sound, but then he finally agreed. "All right, all right. Not even then."

"Thank you."

"I just felt so bad, like what happened with you and Rogan was all my fault, you know? If it hadn't been for me, you never would've met him."

"Oh, please. You need to give that up. Yes, it's possible that without you, Rogan and I would never have met. So what? The point is that no matter how we met, we would have been attracted to each other. Very strongly attracted.

And nature would have probably ended up taking its course. It's not about you. And it's not your fault. So get over yourself."

On Wednesday evening, a week and a half after the disastrous discussion in Rogan's office, Elena stood in that same doorway again.

She waited for him to look up from his computer before she said, "My mom just called. She and my dad are hoping we can come down for Easter. It's a big thing for them. Their first Easter together again…"

Plus, well, she would always think of Easter as the beginning for her and Rogan. Last year, they'd been together at Bravo Ridge. They'd held hands.

And he'd kissed her in Luke's office.

Should she remind him of that?

Would he smile and say he remembered?

Or just go on looking at her the way he was now, his eyes so cool, his expression way too composed. He sat back in his chair. "Why don't you go ahead, you and Michael?"

Tears rose, burning, in the back of her throat. She gulped them down and spoke evenly. "Please, Rogan. I would really like it if you would come with us."

"No, thanks."

"Rogan, I…" What to say next? How to go on from there? He wasn't helping. He was only waiting for her to finish and leave him alone. "I hate this. I really do. This… coolness between us. I wish we could just get past it, you know?" *Get past it.* She winced at her own words. Really, if she was going to try and reach out to him, she needed to come up with something better than *Can't we get past this?*

Too bad she had nothing. She'd pretty much said what

she had to say to him a week and a half before. He either had to pick up the ball.

Or not.

So far, it was always *not*.

He shrugged. "I think you should go to San Antonio for Easter. Go. And enjoy yourself."

Enjoy yourself. Sure.

It was all wrong between them now. And he just didn't want to deal with her.

So all right. She would look on the bright side. Maybe a break wouldn't be such a bad thing. "I think I'll just go ahead then, leave tomorrow. Drive down."

"Have a good time." He turned back to his computer again.

She was officially dismissed.

Fine. She would go to San Antonio for Easter. And she would have a *great* time.

Rogan came home the next evening and they were gone—his wife and his child. And he wanted them back there, with him.

The house seemed empty without them.

He wanted to get in his car or catch the next flight. And be down in San Antonio with Elena and Michael.

But he did nothing to make that happen.

She'd left him a message on the answering machine. "Hi. Just wanted to let you know I'm at my mom and dad's. We had a safe trip." A silence, as she must have debated whether or not to add, "Miss you. See you Monday."

Click. Dial tone. Gone.

He erased the message and went about his evening: dinner, an hour in his office to pay a few bills, channel surfing for a while. A night of fitful sleep.

Saturday went by. And Easter Sunday.

She called Monday morning at seven, while he was sitting at the kitchen table eating breakfast.

"Hi." Her voice was carefully neutral. "How're you doing?"

"No problems," he muttered.

"I was thinking I might stay the week. Mercy invited me to spend some time out at Bravo Ridge. And then, Wednesday or Thursday, I thought I'd go over to the condo. I need to start clearing it out, deciding what to keep and what to sell."

A week without her. The days stretched ahead, empty. Lonely. But then again, how much better was it going to be when she got home? It wasn't like he had all that much to say to her lately.

He would miss Michael. But a week wasn't forever.

"Sounds good," he said. "See you next week," and hung up before she could say another word—before, he realized too late, she had a chance to tell him what day, exactly, she would be back.

The day didn't really matter, he told himself. Friday or next Monday. Or Saturday or Sunday. At the most, it was only seven days.

Seven days when he wouldn't see her face, wouldn't watch that gorgeous dimple appear when she smiled…

Not that she smiled all that much recently.

He knew it was his fault. He knew he should do something about it.

But he only seemed to be making it worse.

He was angry at her. And he just couldn't seem to get past that.

That evening, he stopped at the Highland Park Whole Foods to pick up a few things.

He was in the cereal aisle, reading the back of a granola box, when a woman said, "Rogan. How *are* you?"

He set the box back on the shelf and turned. "Pauline. Hey. Doing great."

"Haven't seen you in a couple of months." Did she look hurt? He supposed that maybe she had a right to be. He'd dropped her off the night Michael was born and never called her again. "You...don't come in the shop anymore." She meant her coffee bar, Perfect Brew. And she was right. He'd purposely avoided any opportunity to run into her.

She was a good person. A nice woman. Attractive. But she had never been the woman for him. Even if he wasn't married now, he wouldn't be considering asking her out again.

He said, "I got married." And held up his ring finger with its thick platinum band.

She blinked. "Oh. Well. Congratulations."

"Thanks." He smiled.

Her answering smile was way too bright. "Well. Better get moving."

"Yeah. Me, too." He rolled on by her, not glancing back.

At home, the house seemed to echo, too big and too quiet. He turned on the kitchen flat-screen TV just to push back the silence as he put his groceries away.

He kept thinking about Pauline. And about the other women he'd dated in the months after that magical week with Elena. Nothing much had gone on with any of them. Inevitably, he would end up comparing them to Elena.

And every one of them fell short.

Which was another reason, he saw now, that he was angry at his wife. After her, after those brief, shining days and nights with her, the freedom he'd waited a decade for had seemed gray and joyless. Down in the darkest part of his heart, he had blamed her for stealing his pleasure in being on his own.

He had blamed her for so much, really, hadn't he?

Even though, in the end, he couldn't see himself married to anyone but her. Even though she was absolutely right for him in all the ways that mattered. Even though when he imagined a life without her, it was an empty life.

As joyless as his life right this moment.

For some reason he didn't understand in the least, he picked up the phone and he called his younger brother.

Niall answered on the second ring. "Hey. Been meaning to call. How's married life treating you?"

"My wife is kind, smart and beautiful. And she can cook. My son is amazing."

"Well, there you go. You're a happy man."

I could be. If I would only let myself be. "I have a question."

"Yeah?"

"How did you see me, after mom and dad died?"

Niall gave a low, dry laugh. "You're kidding, right? I was a mess then, in case you've forgotten."

"No. I haven't forgotten. But that's not my question. What did you think of me?"

"I thought you were the SOB who was always trying to tell me what to do."

"Yeah. Got that message loud and clear."

"And I thought…"

Suddenly, his breath was stuck in his throat. "Yeah? Say it."

Niall backpedaled. "You know, it doesn't matter. We're all grown-up now. We got through it and we all turned out fine."

"Niall."

"What?"

"I'm not calling to get on you. I just want to know what you really thought of me back during the worst times."

"You do. Seriously?"

"I do. Yes."

"Well, all right." Niall paused, as though carefully considering what he was going to say. And then he came out with it. "Sometimes I thought you hated us—me, most of all. That you hated being stuck with us, and with me in particular, since I was the one who gave you the most grief. That you resented the hell out of us and you were angry at us a lot of the time, though with Cormac and Brenda you tried not to show it. You were mad at us just for being there, being your responsibility, now that Mom and Dad were gone." *Anger. Resentment.* There did seem to be a pattern here. "Rogan? Are you going to hang up on me?"

"I'm still here and I'm not hanging up. And you're right. I was angry and resentful. I never hated you, though. I... loved you." As he stumbled over the words, he realized he hadn't said them enough—hardly at all, when you came right down to it. So he said them again. "I *love* you. Present tense."

"Well." Niall cleared his throat. "That's good. I love you, too."

"Also, you turned out great. And I'm proud. So proud of you."

"Yeah?"

"Yeah."

After a minute, Niall asked cautiously, "So you're sure that wasn't too much for you to take?"

"No way. As a matter of fact, it was exactly what I needed to hear."

After Niall, Rogan called Cormac. "I want to take the rest of the week off. Think you can manage without me till next Monday?"

"Not a problem. We're pretty much on schedule." He ran down the projects they had in the works. "Yeah. We're okay. It's tax week, but I'm on top of it. I'm sending the returns off tomorrow."

Rogan knew the tax returns were ready to go. He'd already signed them. "I can get back earlier, if you need me. Just call my cell."

"Fair enough. Where you headed?"

"Elena and the baby are down at the Bravo ranch visiting her sister. Thought I'd fly down, surprise her."

"Can't get along without her, huh?"

"That's about the size of it—and Cormac?"

"What else?"

"You're an excellent brother, a fine business partner and a very good friend. I love you a lot."

"Travel safe," his brother said softly.

"Thanks. I will."

Tuesday morning after breakfast, Elena and Mercy took the kids, a playpen and a basket of toys for Lucas and went out to sit on the front veranda.

It was a pleasant day, warm and getting warmer. But at least there was a nice breeze.

They didn't talk a lot. It was lovely, really, Elena thought. Peaceful. Just sitting there, side-by-side in a matched pair of big, white wooden rockers, the wide Texas sky spread out in front of them, Lucas stacking blocks at their feet. The babies lay in the soft-sided blue playpen together, Serena asleep and Michael gazing dreamily up at the butterfly mobile that Mercy had attached to one of the sides, making happy little giggling sounds to himself.

Elena closed her eyes and let her head fall back. She rocked slow and steady, her thoughts straying where she wished they wouldn't: to Rogan.

Yesterday, he'd hung up before she'd even told him what day she and Michael would be home. Like he couldn't wait to get away from her.

Like he didn't even care if she ever came back to him.

She did not want to grow bitter, to become as angry at him as he continued to be at her. But sometimes she wondered how long a woman could be expected to keep her heart and mind open, to nurture loving feelings for a man who seemed to wish she would simply...disappear?

Just thinking about Rogan depressed her. The problem seemed unsolvable. She wanted to make things better between them. But she didn't know how.

So she was avoiding the problem altogether, staying away from him, hanging out here at Mercy's when she probably should have gone home yesterday, as originally planned. After all, as long as she was here and he was there, the chance of them coming to some kind of peace with each other was pretty much nil.

It's pretty much nil, anyway, said a bleak voice in her head. She heard that voice a lot lately.

And that really brought her down. She'd always thought of herself as a take-charge, problem-solving person. But lately, well, she was seeing that some solutions took two. She couldn't make her marriage work without at least a little help from her husband.

She felt Mercy's hand then, on her bare forearm. Mercy's fingers were warm and firm, reaching across the small distance between their rocking chairs. Elena told herself to count her blessings. She had a beautiful child and the best sister in the world. And a big extended family who loved her as much as she loved them.

Things could be a whole lot worse. She needed to keep that in mind.

The purr of a powerful engine cut through the morning quiet.

Mercy squeezed her·arm. "We've got company."

Elena lifted her head and opened her eyes as the rented Lexus rolled to a stop at the base of the wide front steps. The windows were tinted. She couldn't see who was behind the wheel.

Still, she had the strangest lifting, excited feeling under her breastbone. Weightless as a sunbeam, that feeling, light as a white dove with its wings spread for flight. She knew what it was: hope.

But the feeling changed to something darker, something washed in the harsh burn of rising tears, as her husband emerged from behind the wheel.

Chapter Sixteen

Elena got up from the rocker. She stood tall. She had the silliest urge to smooth her hair, to run her hands down the front of the old jeans she wore.

But she didn't. She simply stood there, waiting.

She had no idea what to say to him. So she didn't say a thing. And maybe that was for the best. Let him try to figure out something to say first, for a change.

He stopped at the foot of the steps, shielded his eyes with his big hand and said, "Hi."

She gave it back to him. "Hi."

He glanced behind her, at her sister. "Mercedes," he said.

Elena heard the rocker creak. Her sister said, "Rogan. How are you?"

"Lonely." He started up the steps.

And her heart was going so fast, like a jackrabbit trapped

inside her chest, beating its strong, swift feet against her rib cage, frantic to get free.

And then he was up on the wide porch with her, between the two central pillars that flanked the steps. He looked good. Fit. In a tan shirt and tan trousers. But up close, she could see the dark shadows of fatigue beneath his eyes.

She wanted to throw her arms around him and never let him go. She wanted to turn and walk away and not look back.

He caught her gaze and held it. His eyes were the warm, vibrant green of the man who had been her lover last May. The man who had brought her tropical flowers and heart-shaped balloons in the middle of the night.

"Elena." His voice was rough, torn-sounding. "Could we have a few minutes alone?"

She had the cruelest urge to do to him what he'd done to her that Sunday more than two weeks before, to look him straight in those clover-green eyes and say, *Can't you see I'm kind of busy here? I don't have time for you now.* But the urge passed. She asked her sister, "Will you keep an eye on Michael?"

"Of course."

Rogan glanced down into the playpen. She watched as a soft smile lifted the corners of his mouth. "Michael. Hey. How're you doing, big guy?"

The baby cooed and giggled, as if he knew his name already—as if he recognized his dad.

Maybe Rogan wanted a few minutes with his son. He hadn't been such a great husband lately, but he was a dedicated dad.

Elena suggested, "Go ahead and hold him. We can talk later."

He looked at her again. "No. Please. Now."

Her face felt hot and her pulse boomed in her ears. "All

right. Let's go inside." She turned and went in through the wide front door. He followed, closing it after him. She went on up the wide staircase, acutely aware of his firm tread behind her.

The door to the room she was using stood open. She led him through.

It was a nice, big room, with lots of light coming in the bow window that looked out over the front grounds. Michael's portable crib stood on the far side of the bed near an antique mahogany bureau. The bed had a white cover with celery-green throw pillows.

She gestured at the two floral-patterned slipper chairs by the bow window. He went and sat down in one. She took the other.

Silence. Except for the roar of her own blood in her ears.

So strange. The two of them, sitting stiffly in the golden wash of morning light. Two married people who had no idea what to say to each other.

Rogan spoke at last. "I've been missing you. So bad."

Coulda fooled me. She sat straighter, stiffer. But at least her heart rate slowed a little.

He had confessed that he'd missed her. That was something. That was…a step.

He tried again. "I treated you wrong. I know I did. I… well, while you were gone, I ran into this woman I dated last year."

"A…woman?"

He nodded. "I was out with her the night that Caleb called to tell me you were at the hospital having Michael. I took her straight to her house, dropped her off and never called her again."

Now her chest felt like some giant fist was squeezing it. She didn't want to hear about him and some other woman. "Rogan. Why are you telling me about some other woman?"

He stared. "But I'm not."

"But you just said—"

"Elena, I swear to you. This isn't about another woman. No way. It's about you. I met this woman I had gone out with, Pauline, in Whole Foods and she said hi and kind of looked hurt that I had never called her again. And I held up my ring finger and said I was married. She congratulated me. And that was all. She rolled her cart one way and I went the other."

He still wasn't making any sense to her. "And I need to know this…why?"

"Because I saw her—and all I could think of was you."

The fist around her heart loosened a fraction. "Me?"

"Yeah." He was looking so young, suddenly. Young and hopeful. "Elena, you're the one. The only one for me. There's no one else. And there won't be. Not only because you're my wife. But because I love you. I don't want to be with anyone but you. I don't want to be free. I honestly don't." He raised his right hand, palm out. "And I swear to you, this is only me talking. Nobody coached me. I haven't spoken to your brother in weeks."

Tears clogged her throat. She sniffed them away with a hard toss of her head. "But you said—"

"I know what I said." He leaned closer. "And I see now. I get it. None of it, all the crap I laid on you, was ever even about you. It was about me. About my bitterness and my resentment when I had to take over raising my brothers and sister after our parents died."

"But wait. I thought that raising your brothers and Brenda was your choice, you know? That it was what you wanted to do."

"No. It was what I felt I *had* to do."

"Not a choice?"

"Sure, yeah. A choice. But a choice I felt forced to make, one I really didn't want." He made a low sound, shook his head. "Your dad as good as called me a hero, that first day I met you, when the three of us went out to lunch together. I was no hero. I was a self-absorbed twenty-one-year-old kid who knew he would never forgive himself if he let the state have his brothers and little sister. So I took them. And I resented them and the hard, slogging job I knew I had ahead of me, raising them. I got it in my head that when Brenda finally went away to college—then, at last, I would have my time to myself…"

She said, gently now, "But the moment you were finally free, you met me."

He chuckled, the sound weighted with irony. "And by then I was so locked into my freedom as my payback, I couldn't see what I could have with you, that you were—and are—the best thing that's ever happened to me. I pushed you away. And then I blamed you when you didn't come running to me to take care of you when you found out you were having my baby. I put it all on you. I had the habit of resenting the ones I loved. I just…went right on with my habit. I transferred my anger and my resentment from my brothers and sister to you." He rose, stood looking down at her in the pool of light from the morning sun. "Pretty messed up, huh?"

She gazed up at him, wondering how such a great guy could have gotten everything so turned around. "Yeah. Pretty messed up—but then again, well, it happens sometimes. We get confused. It all gets twisted."

"And before we know it, we've lost what we want—what we *love*—the most."

"You're right. That can happen."

He stuck his hands in his pockets, as though he didn't quite know what to do with them—or maybe because he was a little afraid to reach for her. His eyes were so soft. "Have I...lost you?"

She gazed up at him. And the lightness was back within her, filling her up. It was more than hope now. It was love. Realized. She held his shining eyes and she told him, "No, you haven't lost me. I'm yours. Always." She said her father's word for it: *"Siempre."*

"Elena..." He said it so softly. Like a prayer.

She rose to stand with him in the wash of morning sun. And her tears rose, too, and she let them. They spilled over. She didn't care. She let them slide, unashamed, down her cheeks. "I was so afraid that you were never going to look beyond your own anger, so afraid we would never have the kind of marriage I've always dreamed of."

"I think we can, Elena. I *know* we can." He dared to reach out then, to touch her cheek, to cradle her upturned face in both of his cherishing hands, to brush away her tears with his warm, rough thumbs. "I love you. With my whole heart, with every part of myself. There's...nothing in the way of that anymore. I swear it to you." He lowered his mouth then.

She lifted hers.

He claimed her lips in a kiss so tender, a kiss that spoke of their lives, unfolding, of the family they had made, the two of them, with Michael. Of the years ahead, filled with laughter and hardship, with struggle, sometimes. And so much joy.

"Will you take me back?" he asked, so gently, so hopefully, when he lifted his mouth from hers.

She smiled up at him through her tears. "Oh, Rogan. Don't you know? I never let you go."

* * * * *

Watch for Travis Bravo's story,
A BRAVO HOMECOMING,
available in November 2011,
only from Silhouette Special Edition.

COMING NEXT MONTH

Available March 29, 2011

SPECIAL EDITION

REQUEST YOUR FREE BOOKS!

2 FREE NOVELS PLUS 2 FREE GIFTS!

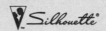

SPECIAL EDITION
Life, Love and Family!

YES! Please send me 2 FREE Silhouette Special Edition® novels and my 2 FREE gifts (gifts are worth about $10). After receiving them, if I don't wish to receive any more books, I can return the shipping statement marked "cancel." If I don't cancel, I will receive 6 brand-new novels every month and be billed just $4.24 per book in the U.S. or $4.99 per book in Canada. That's a saving of at least 15% off the cover price! It's quite a bargain! Shipping and handling is just 50¢ per book in the U.S. and 75¢ per book in Canada.* I understand that accepting the 2 free books and gifts places me under no obligation to buy anything. I can always return a shipment and cancel at any time. Even if I never buy another book, the two free books and gifts are mine to keep forever.

235/335 SDN FC7H

Name	(PLEASE PRINT)	
Address		Apt. #
City	State/Prov.	Zip/Postal Code

Signature (if under 18, a parent or guardian must sign)

Mail to the **Reader Service:**
IN U.S.A.: P.O. Box 1867, Buffalo, NY 14240-1867
IN CANADA: P.O. Box 609, Fort Erie, Ontario L2A 5X3

Not valid for current subscribers to Silhouette Special Edition books.

Want to try two free books from another line?
Call 1-800-873-8635 or visit www.ReaderService.com.

* Terms and prices subject to change without notice. Prices do not include applicable taxes. Sales tax applicable in N.Y. Canadian residents will be charged applicable taxes. Offer not valid in Quebec. This offer is limited to one order per household. All orders subject to credit approval. Credit or debit balances in a customer's account(s) may be offset by any other outstanding balance owed by or to the customer. Please allow 4 to 6 weeks for delivery. Offer available while quantities last.

Your Privacy—The Reader Service is committed to protecting your privacy. Our Privacy Policy is available online at www.ReaderService.com or upon request from the Reader Service.

We make a portion of our mailing list available to reputable third parties that offer products we believe may interest you. If you prefer that we not exchange your name with third parties, or if you wish to clarify or modify your communication preferences, please visit us at www.ReaderService.com/consumerschoice or write to us at Reader Service Preference Service, P.O. Box 9062, Buffalo, NY 14269. Include your complete name and address.

SSE11

Selene wanted nothing to do with the father of her son, Alex; but Aristedes had other plans...that included them.

Read on for an sneak peek from
THE SARANTOS SECRET BABY by Olivia Gates,
available April 2011, only from Harlequin Desire.

"You were right to turn my marriage offer down," Aristedes said.

And Selene found her voice at last, found the words that would not betray the blow he'd dealt her. "Thanks for letting me know. You didn't have to come all the way here, though. You could have just let it go. I left yesterday with the understanding that this case is closed."

Before the hot needles behind her eyes could dissolve into an unforgivable display of stupidity and weakness, she began to close the door.

The door stopped against an immovable object. His flat palm.

"I can't accept that." His voice was low, leashed.

What did her tormentor mean now? Was he ending one game only to start another?

She raised eyes as bruised as her self-respect to his, found nothing there but solemnity and determination.

Before she could voice her confusion, he elaborated. "I never let anything go unless I'm certain it's unworkable. I realize I made you an unworkable offer, and that's why I'm withdrawing it. I'm here to offer something else. A workability study."

She leaned against the door, thankful for its support and partial shield. "Your son and I are not a business venture you can test for feasibility."

His gaze grew deeper, made her feel as if he was trying to delve into her mind, take control of it. "It's actually the other way around. I'm the one who would be tested."

She shook her head. "Why bother? I know—and *you* know—you're not workable. Not with me."

His spectacular eyebrows lowered over eyes she felt were emitting silver hypnosis. "You're right again. Neither you nor I have any reason to believe that isn't the truth. The only truth. It might be best for both you and Alex to never hear from me again, to forget I exist. But then again, maybe not. I'm only asking for the chance for both of us to find out for certain. You believe I'm unworkable in any personal relationship. I've lived my life based on that belief about myself. I never really had reason to question it. But I have one now. In fact, I have two."

Find out what happens in
THE SARANTOS SECRET BABY by Olivia Gates,
available April 2011, only from Harlequin Desire.

Bianca

Una mujer capaz de iniciar una guerra

A Zafar Nejem lo habían llamado de muchas maneras: "jeque errante", "traidor", "bandido moderno"… Pero había llegado el momento de que lo llamaran "Su Majestad". Al subir al trono de Al Sabah, lo primero que hizo fue rescatar a una rica heredera americana, Analise Christensen, de quienes la habían secuestrado en el desierto.

Como Ana estaba prometida al gobernante del país vecino, su presencia debía mantenerse en secreto hasta que Zafar pudiera explicar los motivos de la misma, ya que, en caso contrario, se arriesgaba a que estallara la guerra entre ambos países. Pero al igual que el sol se elevaba sobre las dunas de arena, el deseo prohibido entre Ana y Zafar iba en aumento, poniendo en peligro sus planes.

En el calor del desierto

Maisey Yates

¿EN TU RANCHO O EN EL MÍO?

KATHIE DeNOSKY

Una simple partida de póquer había convertido a Lane en el propietario del rancho Lucky Ace. El único obstáculo que se le presentaba para hacerlo su hogar permanente era la copropietaria, Taylor Scott, que era muy bonita, pero que estaba decidida a quedarse con la propiedad. Para colmo, se había ido a vivir… con él.

Lane solo encontró una solución: jugarse el rancho en otra partida de cartas. Pero hasta entonces… ¿por qué no pasar un buen rato juntos?

Afortunado en el juego y en el amor

¡YA EN TU PUNTO DE VENTA!

Acepte 2 de nuestras mejores novelas de amor GRATIS

¡Y reciba un regalo sorpresa!

Oferta especial de tiempo limitado

Rellene el cupón y envíelo a

Harlequin Reader Service®
3010 Walden Ave.
P.O. Box 1867
Buffalo, N.Y. 14240-1867

¡Sí! Por favor, envíenme 2 novelas de amor de Harlequin (1 Bianca® y 1 Deseo®) gratis, más el regalo sorpresa. Luego remítanme 4 novelas nuevas todos los meses, las cuales recibiré mucho antes de que aparezcan en librerías, y factúrenme al bajo precio de $3,24 cada una, más $0,25 por envío e impuesto de ventas, si corresponde*. Este es el precio total, y es un ahorro de casi el 20% sobre el precio de portada. ¡Una oferta excelente! Entiendo que el hecho de aceptar estos libros y el regalo no me obliga en forma alguna a la compra de libros adicionales. Y también que puedo devolver cualquier envío y cancelar en cualquier momento. Aún si decido no comprar ningún otro libro de Harlequin, los 2 libros gratis y el regalo sorpresa son míos para siempre.

416 LBN DU7N

Nombre y apellido	(Por favor, letra de molde)
Dirección	Apartamento No.
Ciudad	Estado	Zona postal

Esta oferta se limita a un pedido por hogar y no está disponible para los subscriptores actuales de Deseo® y Bianca®.

*Los términos y precios quedan sujetos a cambios sin aviso previo.
Impuestos de ventas aplican en N.Y.

SPN-03   ©2003 Harlequin Enterprises Limited

Resistirse era inútil...

Serena Scott sabía que Finn St George solo podría causarle problemas. Era un hombre impresionante y uno de los mejores pilotos del mundo, sí, pero estaba empeñado en matarse y ella tenía que volver a encauzarlo.

A Finn le encantaba ser un playboy. Al fin y al cabo, disfrutar de mujeres bellas era mucho más placentero que aferrarse a su amargo pasado, pero Serena se resistía a sus encantos y eso hacía que hubiese entre ambos una batalla de deseos. ¿Lograría ella domarlo, o se vería enredada en el sensual poder de su atracción?

Más allá de la culpa

Victoria Parker